ABOUT TIME

Original text © Simona Sparaco
English translation © Howard Curtis 2011

About Time first published in Italian as
Bastardi senza amore in 2010

This edition first published in 2012 by
Pushkin Press
71–75 Shelton Street
London WC2H 9JQ

ISBN 978 1 906548 90 2

Cover Illustration: Henry Rivers
© Henry Rivers 2012

Set in 10 on 13 Monotype Baskerville
by Tetragon
and printed and bound by CPI Group (UK) Ltd, Croydon, CR0 4YY

www.pushkinpress.com

SIMONA SPARACO

ABOUT TIME

Translated from the Italian by
Howard Curtis

PUSHKIN PRESS
LONDON

To my impatient V.
for all the seconds,
all the minutes,
all the hours.

1

"SVEVO, WHY DON'T YOU ever return my calls?"

I've never understood what goes through a woman's head when she ventures on such dangerous terrain.

"I have a lot to do," I reply, my usual impatience clinging to my insides like a monkey.

"You just don't want to."

"If that's how you prefer to look at it."

There's a flash of anger behind her calm smile. I know the taste of this woman's skin, the texture of her private parts, the smell of her hair when the sweat plasters it onto her neck and forehead, even the exact pitch of her moans of pleasure, and yet I can't make out anything in her expression but anger. And I can barely remember her name.

"You're a hopeless case. I really don't know what to do with you."

"Neither do I," I say with a shrug.

At this point, admitting defeat, she stands up. We aren't alone at the table. We're a well-matched group, men on a loose rein looking for fun, plus this girl and her companion in adventure, who seems to be getting on like a house on fire with the Deputy and doesn't appear to have any intention of letting go.

"I'm off. What are you going to do? Are you coming with me?"

"I'll see you at home," the other girl replies, barely looking up.

"Where are you going?" my friend Federico asks her.

She walks away without answering, casting a final glance of disapproval at me before she disappears among the crowd.

She was a dark one. That's what my friends and I call one-night stands who fade into the shadows by the light of day.

"You're turning nasty, Svevo," Federico says ironically. "You're like an old maid." The others echo his laughter.

I know he's right. The fact is, I'm at that time of life when everything starts to turn stale. You must know what I mean. As soon as women feel comfortable with my routine, I start getting restless. It's flattering at first, the way they look at me. I think they see me as a dominant male, the kind who'll protect the nest. It's all a question of nature, it's written in the DNA of our species. Then, gradually, the excitement gives way to impatience, and none of it seems to matter any more: the colour of their hair, the smell of their skin, their perfect smiles, their well-toned thighs and arses. After a while, their gorgeous, Botoxed faces become redundant, superfluous, and that's when, as my best friend says, I turn nasty.

Happy Hour continues, and I'm pretty sure some other dark one will jump on our merry-go-round sooner or later, but for the moment it's enough to know there's someone sitting with the Deputy, pending the pleasant evening I've laid on for him.

We're in a bar in a square in Rome, a place where You have a long memory, and there opposite us, imposing and golden, is the Temple of Hadrian, but nobody seems to be paying any attention to its mute presence, nobody's succumbing to its charms, everybody's busy with seductive games of another kind entirely.

Amid all the pleasantries, I glimpse a group of young girls who look as if they're out for a good time: the bright lipstick, the high heels, their newly matured attractions, the mobile phones that never stop ringing. They stay close to their older friends, chattering, laughing, playing with their hair. They may only just have come of age, they probably think the NASDAQ is a neurological disease and Bush a brand of detergent, and yet they excite me. Their skin, their hair, the delicacy of their curves, the first coat of polish on their thin nails: there's something indescribable about their charm, the nonchalant way they move, unaware of the fact that they'll never be as beautiful as this again and that they'll soon be torturing themselves with pointless plastic surgery in an attempt to preserve that advantage.

Suddenly I have the impression the temple is looking at me, reading my thoughts. Its beauty is timeless: You've been eating into its majestic columns for centuries, but You haven't succeeded in tarnishing its charm, which actually grows out of all proportion every time You take a bite out of it.

The evening is just getting started, we have dinner booked at a terrace restaurant in central Rome. The usual round of introductions, all those people it's useful to say hello to. With some people you just have to know the right button to push, and I pride myself that I was born knowing that. Sometimes all it takes is a compliment, a well-timed joke, anything to put them at their ease, make them believe you have the solution to their problems in your pockets. The sly, merry expression on the face of my friend the Deputy, as he emerges from the toilet wiping his nostrils, confirms to me I've got it right again, and tomorrow, at the office, we may well receive the phone call we've been

11

waiting for. If we get those building permits, the director will owe me a few favours.

Amid the monosyllables and the laughter, a stunning woman appears. She glides past us, with a male acquaintance I've never bothered with before, but who's now suddenly turned into a dear friend.

"Long time no see! How are you?"

I think I've found my dark one.

I'm introduced to her, and she seems quite shy at first.

"I love this city, it's so stimulating, like an open-air museum." That's the first thing she says to me, in a pronounced Milanese accent. There's not a line on her face, not the smallest defect. Whoever designed her made sure all the optional extras were built in, just as you'd expect of a limited edition.

She's almost fifteen years younger than me, and as I stare at her I'm thinking of the quickest way to get into her knickers, though I know that's a fairly despicable attitude. I realize I made a big mistake, thinking she was shy, when the evening ends up with her standing almost naked in front of my bed.

An olive complexion, the kind I like, and an indecent quantity of brown curly hair tumbling over breasts so perfect she must have had them done. Did she? I'll find out soon enough. She's wearing what I think are real lace knickers, quite tasteful really, and she doesn't seem to have any intention of taking off her stiletto-heeled boots for the moment. I suppose she thinks they're some kind of armour. From the way she purses those petrol-pink lips she seems ready for battle.

I like studying every detail, every centimetre of her body, as if she were a valuable object I was contemplating buying. My only overt reaction is to smile, to show I'm pleased, and she blushes. I suppose she feels like Botticelli's Venus: I'm transforming her, my eyes are the most delicate brushes that have ever caressed her body. I know this lingering scrutiny is starting to drive her crazy, but I'm curious to see how far she'll go, how long it'll take before she at last yields to my gaze and feels obliged to make the first move.

Instead of which, she surprises me: still smiling, she slowly gets dressed again, leaving me like that, lying on the bed. She's like a jeweller closing the casket after revealing the price of the gems. Unfortunately for her, I have no intention of yielding, or of reaching for my wallet, and as she dresses, I equally slowly undress.

She can't help it, she finds the whole thing amusing, but not enough to get her to join me between the sheets, she prefers to sit down in the leather armchair facing the bed. She starts playing distractedly with the remote that controls the blinds over the windows, and when she inadvertently raises them, she's met by the view from my apartment. She's enchanted by the lights of central Rome, so much so that she completely forgets about me lying there naked on the bed. After a few moments of total silence, she turns and says, "Thank you."

"For what?"

"For showing me Rome from here."

I wasn't expecting that. I never thought the view of the Castel Sant'Angelo could cast such a spell on her. I'm about to reply, to start a conversation, but she turns and asks me, "Are you renting, or do you own this gem?"

That seems harsh. I tell her I got a good deal on it, get proudly up off the bed and walk to the kitchen stark naked. I'm ready to open the Dom Pérignon I keep chilled for difficult cases like her. I come back to the bedroom and uncork it behind her. She turns, a bit startled, then smiles.

"When it's like this, Rome deserves a toast, don't you think?" I say, shaking the bottle over her.

I slide my fingers over her silky skin, now wet with champagne, until I get to her breasts. She *has* had them done, as I guessed, but they're just as exciting as if they were real. A grin, the grin of someone savouring victory, comes to life on my face. She must wish I was more passionate, she must wish she could measure my desire by the insistent touch of my fingers, but I continue to keep my distance, touching her lightly with only one hand, exploring hesitantly, and I know that very soon, in a very few seconds, she'll be the one to sweep me off my feet, and I'll find myself thrown down on the bed, intoxicated with her scent, panting, beneath a wild riot of curly hair.

When it's over I turn into a different man.

I've been living with my mood swings since I was a little boy, since before all the nights spent in clubs and the binges and the after-effects of coke, since before I became successful. Once my testosterone has exploded in orgasm, my mind makes room for accounts and work projects and next day's schedule, and in all this rapid channel-flicking there's no place for a woman's reflections.

She's lit a cigarette and from her sighs I sense she'd really like to chat. Which is what she does, starting with her work, then the fog in Milan. She tells me she'd like to move. Doesn't she know that's the kind of talk that scares a man off? Then she compliments me on my apartment, she says she's never seen so many gadgets in one place. "It must have cost you a fortune," she says. "Why do you need a TV in the bathroom?"

With some women it's actually too easy, a few special effects and you get the same respect from them that you get when you shake someone's hand with a couple of banknotes rolled up in yours. They open all doors.

She loses a few more points when she starts walking naked around the outside of the bed, still holding her cigarette, and peers at my things. My clothes will all be smelling of smoke soon. The last straw is when she presses a button and activates the shelf under the bedside table, which rises hydraulically to reveal some spirits and a little cocaine. I always keep some there to liven up those evenings that finish in this apartment, and activating that mechanism is something that always strikes them dumb with amazement.

"What's this?" she says with a laugh. "Is this where you hide the entertainment?"

"Put it back the way it was."

"I'd like to try some," she says, although from the way she handles it I know this certainly isn't her first time, and besides, I've never found initiations exciting.

"Look, it's late. Come back to bed."

Luckily, she likes playing the role of the obedient child. At last she stops messing about with my things. "Aren't you afraid the police will raid this place?" she asks as she waits for the shelf to descend and everything to go back into position.

"Why should they?"

She lies down again on the bed and lights another cigarette. Again that bit of ash about to fall, which really annoys me.

When, between one drag and another, she asks me to tell her something about my life, I pretend I've fallen asleep and reply with an irritated mutter. Finding ways to avoid conversation is a trick I inherited from my father, and all at once, in the half-light of the room, his image appears in front of me like a faded slide. His unmistakable sulk reminds me of our dinners together, when I would nod wearily as I looked at the worn-out kitchen utensils, the untidy dining table, where he kept his papers, and the dismal dried flowers in the yellow earthenware vases and thought about the Futurist paintings I was studying at school, the speed of a brand-new sports car, the exalting of pleasure and youth in Oscar Wilde. I couldn't wait for him to let me go so that I could get back to the stern, irreproachable rhythms of the teachers he'd entrusted me to after throwing in the towel. I much preferred the sanitized corridors during those interminably slow, mind-numbingly boring hours of punishment to the airless atmosphere of home. I wanted to knock down those four walls, turn my life upside down, and I was sure that sooner or later I would: one day I'd leave school, along with all the other wild kids, and find my own path, I'd become master of my own time and invest it in the race to succeed.

These are the thoughts that fill the muffled silence of the room, the conviction that his inability to love me was lucky for me, because if I hadn't taken that course, I wouldn't be the kind of man I am today. I'd probably still be living in Turin, trying to drum up business for his cash-strapped legal practice. We weren't meant to live together. Our relationship has always been precariously balanced, a matter of cautious, moderate gestures, as if our worlds, so remote one from the other, have to be kept at a distance, under strict control, to avoid collapse. I'm still convinced that the key to everything is control, control of every moment, even the most unpredictable, and that it was control that stopped me going mad, stopped me being swallowed up by the emptiness that swallowed up my father in the end.

Order is the basis of my work. Order is mathematics, and numbers never let you down, it's not in their nature. You just have to see me to understand: I'm at the top of an investment company, calculations and opportunities are inextricably entwined if you want to be part of that narrow circle of people who hold the right cards in their hands. I can't help being pleased with the aces I've been dealt lately, and the gorgeous girl who's now asleep beside me is a consequence of them. When the desire for sex returns, I don't have to do anything but start kissing her again, allowing myself to get excited by her ready responses, by the fact that she offers no resistance, and at the same time the thought makes its way inside me that she'll soon be gone, and that in my bedroom, as in my life, order will eventually be restored.

As for You, Father Time, You're watching me all the while, as discreet as a guardian angel. You let me carry on, You let me believe that You're mine to command, whereas in fact You're eating away at me every day, almost imperceptibly, and I'm sure You can't wait to enjoy the spectacle of my defeat.

2

A STEAMING CUP OF COFFEE and a telephone number, written on what looks like a pair of knickers: that's the visiting card I find next to my empty bed the following morning.

It's seven o'clock, although my watch says 7.05. I always put it forward by five minutes to make sure I arrive on time, or even in advance. I've always been particular about getting ready in the morning, that's why I wake up two hours before I start work. There are things I like to do calmly: choosing my clothes and making sure the colours match, having my breakfast, reading the newspapers.

By 8.30, according to my watch, my driver, Antonio, is waiting for me outside my building. My baby, a dark-grey Aston Martin Vanquish, is in the garage, I'll be using it tonight. It'd be too restless for the morning traffic—and besides, with Antonio driving, I can get stuff done on the way to the office: organizing my day, checking my e-mails, looking through a few documents.

Our company's head office is in a period building overlooking the Tiber. Paola, the switchboard operator, greets me at the door, a bit embarrassed as she furtively closes the fashion magazine she's been leafing through. I remember she was planning to start a diet, so I tell her she must have lost a few kilos because she's looking really good. Predictably, she reacts with a big smile.

The delivery man has just brought in a package of disinfectant wipes for the director. I tell Paola to make sure it corresponds to the order. The director couldn't live without his disinfectant wipes. He's declared war on germs and bacteria, it's a kind of obsession, an extreme form of hypochondria, even though he's an intelligent, far-sighted man, a real bulldog. I'm due to speak to him later about those building permits.

Now my secretary Elena comes up to me, two dark, sympathetic eyes beneath an impeccable bob. She looks much younger than she really is, which is about thirty. "Don't forget your appointment at ten for the Righini business," she tells me as we enter my office.

My eye falls on her wristwatch, and I smile: she's decided to adopt my trick of putting it forward by five minutes, just to keep us in sync. She's already opened and closed the windows to let a bit of air into the fanatical tidiness of the office: a spacious mahogany desk, two elegant ostrich-leather armchairs. Her efficiency is a good match for my concern with perfection.

"They've already called more than once, the names are on your desk. Oh, and Signora Campi was looking for you a few minutes ago…"

She's barely had time to mention her name when Barbara Campi, the marketing director, comes in.

"Don't bother to knock," I say, greeting her with an ironic smile, then give Elena a little nod. She leaves us alone and I sit down behind my desk.

Barbara is holding a newspaper, she looks impatient. "Have you read this?"

"Yes, if you're referring to the article about us in the *Sole*. Don't tell me you've come just to ask me that."

"Oh, I'm sorry, Signor Romano, I thought you'd missed it," she says, her lips curling in a grimace. "Silly of me to think a man of your calibre could miss an article at nine in the morning, wasn't it?"

"No need to be sarcastic. Just because I'm a man doesn't mean I'm unprepared."

I'm teasing her as usual, I know she thinks of herself as a modern feminist and is convinced women are superior to men, and other bullshit like that.

Continuing in the same vein, I look for a compliment I could give her. "You look different," I say. "You must have had a good weekend."

"It's the latest thing in cosmetics," she says, stroking the outsides of her eyes with her fingers. "I didn't think you'd notice."

"You don't need it. I've told you a thousand times I should call the World Wildlife Fund, you're almost an extinct species."

Actually, I doubt there's any cream so advanced it could give her a charm she's never possessed. It strikes me she's been overdoing the nips and tucks lately: she's starting to have the typical clown-like smile of women who've had facelifts.

"Liar," she retorts. "It's men like you who could convince all the women in the world to move to Mars."

"You really know how to put the knife in. What kind of man am I?"

"You should know, Svevo. You're a flatterer, you're vain, and you're completely untrustworthy as a human being."

"In other words I'm a bastard. I can't make up my mind if you're trying to lose your job here or declaring your undying love for me."

She smiles. "Luckily Mars isn't so far these days."

Barbara has been working in this company for much longer than I have, which has allowed her a certain familiarity from the start. She's very good in her field and the director respects her for her commitment. Nothing seems to exist for her outside this office. And yet she's married and has a ten-year-old son, although she's certainly not one of those mothers you see running around in a car all day, taking their children to school or a five-a-side football game.

Before she leaves, she makes a sarcastic comment about the latest political scandal to hit the newspapers. She loves slagging off other people, especially if she thinks you're going to do the same. She usually finds a common target to get you on her side, and the choice is never random, it's always been carefully thought out. When she spits poison, she purses her lips and her nostrils flare: she reminds me of a python, though I assume she thinks I'm the same as her. "He's history," she says if it's someone we know, especially if it's someone we do business with who could threaten our advantage. She scrutinizes me, half closing her eyes, waiting for a sign of approval. If I feel like it, I nod.

As soon as Barbara leaves the room, Elena comes in and hands me an envelope and a still-sealed ream of paper.

I unwrap the paper first and sniff it. I like the smell of new things. The interior of a car in a showroom, cashmere wrapped in tissue paper, leather shoes that haven't been worn yet. Everything's so spotless at the beginning, so full of promise.

Next, I turn to the envelope. It's from the director.

I open it.

Inside, there are some photographs. They're from last night, and they show our friend the Deputy in poses somewhat unsuited to his position, like strutting with his trousers down around his knees, snorting cocaine. With his toothpick-thin legs, he looks more like a chicken than a peacock. And talking of chickens, the accompanying note includes one of the director's favourite observations: "Romano, did you know that in prehistoric times it wasn't unusual for the eohippus, the ancestor of the horse, to be the prey of the pterodactyl, the ancestor of the hen? Can you imagine a horse being eaten by a hen? We're in constant evolution, my dear Romano, and history teaches us to be on the alert, to beat the others to the draw. Remember, a man you can blackmail is easy prey."

As far as timing is concerned the director is second to none, and he's never had too many qualms when it comes to obtaining what he wants from people.

I'm about to call him, but before I have time to lift the receiver the telephone rings, startling me.

"Signor Romano, your father's on the line, should I put him through?"

"My father?" I echo, surprised.

"Yes, your father."

He must need a loan, that's the only explanation that comes to mind. He rarely telephones me, and when he does our conversations are usually full of long, embarrassing silences. At the end of every call, to avoid another one, which might be even more painful, I arrange for a large bank transfer, hoping that'll keep him off my back for a while.

"Svevo? It's me. How are you?"

The hoarse, cavernous voice echoes in my mind like a childhood song, but only for a few seconds, because the nostalgia fades

23

immediately, leaving me irritable and anxious to hang up and get on with my work. I glance at my watch, then at my diary, and sigh.

"Fine," I reply.

"Good," he says. "I'm glad."

"Is there a particular reason you've called? I'm a bit behind."

"Oh, you, you're always behind."

Then silence again. A silence that chokes any words at birth. Even a monosyllable would feel inappropriate in comparison with this silence. And yet I can sense there's something he wants to tell me, I can tell it from the way he's breathing, slowly and noisily. There's pride in that sound.

"Your cousin's graduating," he says at last, as if that's any concern of mine. He's just beating about the bush, I know he'll get to the point sooner or later.

"Good."

"Yes."

I imagine dinners at my mother's sister's: the smell of boiled chicken that gets into your clothes, my two cousins, in their early twenties, going on about their little lives, my aunt nodding, as stiff as ever, in a permanent state of mourning. They're all so distant from me, I'd be very surprised if they ever talked about me.

"I'm not asking you to come to the graduation."

"I have a lot of things to do."

"I know you've bought a new house... A villa in Cortona, isn't it?"

I don't think he's trying to invite himself. I think he wants a loan, he's probably got a few creditors after him.

"I'm renovating it. I don't know when it'll be ready. Look, I really have to dash."

"OK. Bye then."

"Bye."

The call leaves me with a sense of unfinished business, which I try to shake off by calling Elena on the intercom and asking her to take care of the bank transfer. She doesn't demur when she hears the figure, though she must think it's a serious matter this time. I only hope she hurries up about it.

I go back to my diary to catch my breath. One page follows another in a regular, unceasing rhythm. There's something corresponding to every hour: an appointment, a lunch, a meeting. I'm sure You've looked at me sometimes: hard at work, convinced that being productive means knowing how to structure time, making sure that every action is channelled into a pre-arranged schedule, delegating effectively, making full use of the waiting periods by avoiding pointless meetings that are of no professional benefit. I'm sure You've also noticed my obsequious attitude to the director as we walk together to the conference room, with his hand on my shoulder and my head tilted, listening with great interest to his admonitions and suggestions.

"Please, Romano, I'm counting on you to see this business through," he whispers in my ear in that slightly paternal tone of his. "Righini is in your hands, it's an important acquisition."

The director walks beside me, and I nod and look at him with eyes full of gratitude. Why are You surprised? He was the one who introduced me to the people who matter in this city. And what about the expression on my face when I sit down at the table to negotiate? That gleam in my eyes is pure competitiveness, our daily bread. My rapid way of speaking, my thoughts constantly pursuing new strategies, and at the end of the meeting the mobile phone that starts ringing again, bringing more appointments I can't be late for. Distances have been wiped out, dear Father Time, and You can't do anything about it. Technology allows us to do everything in an instant, we're always ready to receive information from anywhere in the world.

"Mazzoli, calling from New York."

Elena on speakerphone.

"Thanks," I reply, and lift the receiver. "Hi, how are things? Yes, go on… Absolutely not. It's already been sent and should be there by now… Of course… And don't forget Wednesday evening. Everything's all set up… We'll talk about it… Yes, of course… See you soon."

When I put the phone down, I notice my mother staring at me from the photo frame on the bookshelf. I can't remember her, it's pointless for me even to try. My memories of her are fading year by year, just like that photograph, which shows her in her wedding dress, mouth open in a smile of delight. I think it was that smile that bewitched my father. And I think it's because of that smile that he's never got over her death.

My diary reminds me that this evening I have to go and collect Gaëlle, who's flying in from Paris. I pick up the phone and call her. I'll come for her at nine and take her to dinner with some friends at a restaurant that was only opened last month, and to round out the evening I've booked a table in one of the best clubs in town. It's only what she'd expect.

I imagine her nodding at her mobile phone with that aristocratic pout of hers, crossing her legs in a way that's as arousing as it's artificial. As far as I'm concerned, she's the embodiment of beauty and sensuality. Feminine, self-composed, able to stay in control even after an evening fuelled by coke and alcohol.

We met in London, when I was there on a business trip. I spotted her in a club in the West End, under the coloured glare of spotlights. A tight-fitting black sweatshirt, hair gathered in a glossy ponytail. Not a single imperfection, skin like a little girl's, full lips curled in a cute grin. She came to our table to greet an actor who was with us, and as soon as she saw me she started staring at me quite openly. When I stood up to go to the toilet, I felt a hand pulling me by my belt. She smiled at me and told me to take her away. Gaëlle never asks, she smiles. And her smile is the sweetest invitation to go crazy that you could ever hope to receive.

"Remember to wash the car, Stefano, I need it for tonight," I say to the garage owner over the phone before I get back to work.

At the end of the day, usually between seven and eight, I go to the gym, it's become a habit and I never skip a session if I can help it. The gym is the one place where I keep to all my good resolutions. I go there and lift weights, surrounded by mirrors, which appeals to my vanity. I push my muscles to the limit, making sure I reach the targets I've set myself. For the biceps, four sets of twenty, ten kilos each. My mind empties. I start another set of twenty, I feel pleased with myself, my thoughts are weightless, I'm regenerated.

Before dinner, I finally meet my baby. She's waiting for me at the back of the garage. Washed and polished for the occasion, even more gorgeous than the last time I saw her. She has a perfection that no woman, not even Gaëlle, could ever aspire to.

And it's in my baby that I pull up outside the hotel. Gaëlle emerges through the main door, looking every inch a diva, and the roar of the 460-horsepower engine is joined by the echo of her heels on the paving stones. She comes to me, lightly touches my face with her fingertips, and with an air of intrigue whispers, "*Merci, mon cher.*" Then she gets in the car, leaving me with an idiotic smile on my face.

I've always let Gaëlle treat me like shit. The truth of the matter is, she drives me wild and she knows it. Self-controlled, aloof, sometimes almost mechanical, just like my Aston Martin, she knows exactly what gets me. The more elusive she is, the more I want her. She says she'll call me back, then disappears for weeks without a trace. She's the only woman who's able to keep my interest alive, one of those women who have the spirit of conquest in their blood. And on that basis, we've struck the right balance, we've learnt how to get along.

At the restaurant, I can't take my eyes off her, and I don't think I'm the only one. A stunning face, with the kind of casual, involuntary beauty that verges on perfection, two icy blue eyes you just can't escape if they glance in your direction. She's wearing bright lipstick and has a simple but classy hairdo. She jokes with my friends, letting her head fall back when she laughs, her eyes lighting up with mischief. There isn't the slightest suspicion of a line around her eyes. She likes to joke with her girlfriends about the preventive effects of Botox: she makes it seem like an innocent game.

"What kind of dessert do you suggest, Svevo?" she asks me in her captivating French accent.

"Yes, go on, Svevo, recommend a little dessert!"

Federico is teasing me, but his presence makes everything more familiar. We understand each other perfectly, sometimes all we need is a smile. We're on the same wavelength. He's probably thinking the same thing I am right now: that it would take an artist to paint the group at this table. Two blonde models who seem to have come straight from a painting by Degas, elegant, ageless ballerinas, and the two of us, young and attractive, smiling brazenly like sheikhs. With a bit of coke circulating in our veins we feel indestructible.

The restaurant is luxurious and a bit unusual. At the back of the room, behind a large pane of glass, there's a wall of rock with little circles of stones embedded in it according to some geometrical pattern, it must be some kind of Zen idea—you find those stones everywhere these days. Attractive waitresses parade nonchalantly between the tables in their gorgeous blue-green kimonos, with their hair gathered in buns, smiling at whoever's turn it is, in this case Federico, who tells me with his eyes that he's crazy about this place. I care a lot about the mood of the people around me.

Gaëlle is enjoying being the centre of attention, but she never takes her eyes off me. In the car on the way to the club after dinner, she whispers a few exciting fantasies in my ear, then leans back in her seat, amused.

"Can you stop looking at me like that?" she says, lighting a cigarette and blowing the smoke into the air.

"Are you trying to provoke me?"

"I just want to let off steam."

"And I want to see you dance."

I slip a couple of grams in her purse and tell her to be good.

In the car park, before getting out, as usual I check that everything's neat and tidy. She's let a bit of ash fall on her seat, I seem doomed always to go for women who smoke. As I give my baby a little clean, Gaëlle doesn't miss the opportunity to tease me. So I grab her by the arm and kiss her roughly. I'm about to slip my hand inside her knickers, just to make it clear that nobody jokes with me, but before I can do that she pushes me angrily back inside the car.

From the outside I guess I'm a pretty reprehensible specimen. I like touching my baby's steering wheel and running my fingers over the slightly rough stitches of the leather while Gaëlle's lips move up and down without stopping. I like it when the insignificant people who are waiting in line outside the club move aside to let us pass. I like the big white leather sofas in the private area and our women, always a little tipsy, jumping on them for fun. Gaëlle dancing on the glass table and half the club watching her wiggling her hips like a professional go-go dancer. Federico letting his ear be licked by a young blonde as he knocks back one shot of tequila after the other. And me being carried away by the music, until I feel like all the others and stop being disgusted by them. When you come down to it, we're all human, we all go crazy when the rhythm is in time with our heartbeats and the club becomes our world and we turn into one single entity dancing.

3

I'VE ALWAYS BEEN AFRAID of planes. Maybe it's some kind of trauma from my childhood. What scares me is the thought of being trapped in a pressurized box at a height of ten thousand metres and a speed of almost a thousand kilometres an hour, without any control over what's happening. In a situation like that, I feel it's more necessary than ever to take charge of time, to know how much of it we'll take to reach our destination, and exploit every last second of it. That's the only way I can stop my mind from getting the better of me.

It's Friday afternoon and I'm at the airport with a group of friends, waiting to board a plane for Paris, where Gaëlle is waiting for me. We've been invited to a party for the French Oscars or something like that. I'm pacing restlessly between the check-in desks. I've put the hands of my watch five minutes back, to be in sync with the airport clocks. I've bought all the magazines I can, hoping they'll help me keep my mind occupied during the two-hour flight. One hour and fifty-five minutes, to be precise.

I've booked a seat by myself, an aisle seat in the fifth row, because I don't like chatting, it makes me lose my concentration. On top of all that, Federico has to talk business with a daddy's boy he's been working on for a few weeks now, and has also brought along a couple of Romanian women togged out in designer clothes from head to foot.

Going through security, one of the Romanian women is asked to remove her boots because they've set off the metal detector. She loses her temper, and starts sounding off about how pointless the whole procedure is. I feel embarrassed even though I've only just met her. Federico tries to intervene, but the bitch won't calm down, she even turns for support to the person in the queue behind her, a young woman with a little girl asleep in her arms.

"Do I look like a terrorist? I mean, I ask you… They've got it in for me, that's obvious. Do you really think I look like a terrorist?"

The woman with the little girl is unfazed. In a calm, seraphic tone of voice she replies, "You can't even say for certain that people who look like terrorists are actually terrorists."

The Romanian woman is taken aback, she certainly wasn't expecting an answer like that, but she quietens down and takes off her boots.

I look away, and my eye falls on the little girl the woman in the queue is holding with such care. The child is probably only about one, or maybe a little older, and has just opened her eyes, awoken by her mother gently stroking her hair. Still half-dazed, she allows herself to be put down at the request of the security staff, then waits patiently for her mother to collect the luggage and take her in her arms again.

The woman must be about the same age as me, judging from the skin on her face, the maturity of her expression, her eloquent eyes. I wouldn't call her beautiful, but there's something attractive about her long neck, the elegant way she holds herself. She has red hair, a haze of red hair, freckles on her face and between her breasts, large smooth lips, clear-cut features, prominent cheekbones. Her eyes have an undefined colour similar to those of the little girl she's holding in her arms. And the little girl herself is almost insanely beautiful. She's fallen asleep again, cradled by the devoted love her mother gives off like a perfume, a scent of milk and tenderness that overwhelms me on the escalator.

We head for the gate. Federico walks ahead quickly, along with the rest of the group, while I drop behind, still watching the woman and the girl. "Come on, Svevo, get a move on," he calls to me, moving away.

The woman is walking slowly, her daughter's little legs dangling by her side. To that sleeping little creature, her mother is a universe, her broad shoulders are the limits of space. She whispers sweet words to her, in a reassuring tone. Those that reach me evoke a jumbled series of impressions: the hay in a stable, a juice stain on a worn tablecloth, an embrace in the dead of night, a hand passing through sweaty hair.

I think I hate children. Basically, they're just little parasites, never satisfied with what you give them. The fact is, I can't bear the idea of someone depending totally on me, like a dog. Children die if you don't feed them, cry if you shout at them, copy you even when you behave like an idiot. The children I've never had would probably have been little monsters.

Federico stops in front of a poster advertising an expensive watch. "This is your next present to me," he says ironically, and for a moment I lose sight of them. Then, just as I'm about to walk right past them, I see them again. They've stopped by a postcard stand. For an instant, a slight but disturbing jolt spreads through my chest like hot liquid: the woman with the red hair, now holding a postcard in her hand, notices me and gives me a rapid glance which makes me feel naked. She has a serious expression on her face, but her eyes are smiling, as if they were speaking an unknown language.

"Did you hear what I said? You could easily afford this. Come on now, don't be stingy!"

Almost without realizing it, I've come level with Federico, who gives me a humorous slap on the back and says, "Hurry up or we'll miss the plane."

By the time we get to our gate, which is B10, I've lost sight of them again. I don't even know why I'm so determined to see them, the woman isn't really my type. I've never liked red hair, or women over thirty with lines around their eyes, or even the faded colour of the sweater she's wearing. I'm the kind of person who cares about such things. And anyway, I have a plane to catch, and my fear to keep under control.

"Your attention, please. Alitalia flight Z245 to Paris is now boarding. I repeat: Alitalia flight Z245 to Paris is now boarding."

The hostess's words are delivered in such a husky, sensual voice that I'm actually distracted for a while. The girl is quite a looker, too: if she went into the pilot's cabin, she'd probably cause the instrument panel to seize up. I'm just getting to my feet when the woman with the little girl in her arms once again appears ahead of me. She's moving quite slowly, and I suspect she's afraid of waking the girl. I offer to help her with her luggage but she thanks me and says she's fine, she doesn't need any help. As a courtesy, I pretend to be touched by the sleeping child, give her a very forced smile, and wish her a pleasant journey. And now suddenly everything slows down, and my attention is caught by an apparently insignificant detail: the little girl rubbing her angelic face against the woman's neck, as if looking for a shelter in which to sleep more soundly. I'm troubled, almost annoyed, so I grab my bag and push forward as much as I can.

A moment later, it all passes. I'm swallowed up by the flow of the queue at the boarding gate, and the woman disappears among the other passengers.

Once on the plane, a bigger problem awaits me: confronting my anxiety, which is starting to increase at an unacceptable speed. My first instinct is to get off, I'm sure we're heading for a disaster, we're going to crash, I can't breathe. I imagine tomorrow's headlines: *Sixty Passengers and No Way Out.* There's my name in capital letters, with the word *Dead* next to it. Svevo Romano is dead. The plane crashed in the Alps, they found my body still sitting in its seat with the belt fastened. Some are starting to speculate about the circumstances of the accident, my lovers mourn, remembering our nights of sex, my mood swings, how much of a bastard I could be. Some even say: When you come down to it, dying was the only thing he still had left to do.

I feel as if I'm going mad, and yet on the surface everything's fine. I'd like to beg the hostess to let me off, but I don't have the guts. All I can do is resort to one of the things I always use to ward off bad luck.

I'm obsessed with the number five, although obsession isn't quite the right word. I call it my joker, the thing I use to overcome small glitches on a journey, when a valve cracks and the whole mechanism seizes up. It doesn't happen often but it happens, and five is a ritual that comes to my aid, like a prayer. Before sitting down in my seat I count to five. Once seated, trying not to attract attention, I tap the little table in front of me five times, and then, almost childishly, repeat the number five, five times, as I force myself to fasten my seat belt.

I clear my head and try to think rationally. The flight is only one hour and fifty-five minutes, I keep telling myself. I've planned every second and now I'm ready to close my eyes and take off.

One hour and fifty-five minutes.

"We would like to show you some of the safety features of this plane."

One hour and fifty-five minutes.

"An oxygen mask will automatically fall from the compartment above your heads."

One hour and fifty-five minutes.

"Cabin crew, prepare for take-off."

One hour and fifty-five minutes.

We're in the air.

Now at last the warning light goes out, which means I can loosen my belt. I even start to feel a bit more relaxed. I gradually ease my grip on the arms of my seat. We've pierced the sky at high speed and now, as we gain height, the plane even seems to have slowed down.

Outside the window, the sky is so dark, it's swallowed up all the stars. I have to ignore the aisle to my left, which becomes increasingly narrow and oppressive.

I'm getting ready to devote twenty minutes to my first item of reading material, as planned, when the light goes on again unexpectedly.

Apparently, we have to fasten our seat belts again, even though there hasn't been the slightest touch of turbulence.

I turn to Federico and ask for an explanation. His answer is worse than a death sentence.

"We're landing," he says. "We'll be in Paris in ten minutes."

We'll be in Paris in ten minutes.

Paris. In ten minutes.

It's not possible. One hour and fifty-five minutes. I haven't even had time to open my first magazine and we're already about to land.

"Are you joking? What did you say we're doing?"

"What do you mean? Don't mess about… We're arriving in Paris."

It isn't a joke, the plane really is losing height, my ears are getting bunged up. One hour and fifty-five minutes. How is it possible? My heart is beating faster, the plane itself seems to be going faster. It descends, it keeps descending, and I have the impression that everything around me has inexorably speeded up.

At first I think it's one of the effects of fear: I know time and space can be distorted when I look at the world through the lens of my anxiety. I remember a sentence I read in some book or other: "That which is far in time appears imminent, there is only the present." But then all it takes is a moment when you start to lose control and nothing matters any more, except the instinct for survival. And this moment comes without warning, when I realize that time going crazy like this can't be the result of my mind, it's too real, it's actually happening. I unfasten my seat belt and leap to my feet.

One hour and fifty-five minutes. What happened to all those minutes?

"No!" I scream.

One of the hostesses comes to my aid, a blonde girl with glasses, who looks even more scared than I am. Maybe she's afraid I'll hit her, or that I plan to throw the whole plane into a panic, or open the emergency door.

It's pointless, I can't regain control. The girl looks at me indulgently, she's talking to me, but I can't make out what she's saying, her voice sounds weirdly distorted. The passengers are looking at me pityingly. Some have even risen from their seats. Federico is dismayed and embarrassed at the same time, he's never seen me in this state. "Svevo, what's happening to you? We're landing.

There, look, we're almost on the ground. Calm down, we've arrived in Paris."

The minutes and seconds are getting all mixed up and he's asking me to calm down. The noises fade. I see the stewardess's lips moving, but can't hear what she's saying. All I can hear now is my own breathing, which gradually slows down, until I surrender to the push of her slender arms.

"There's no danger," I hear her distorted voice say, and then I feel the plane touch down, it taxis for what seems like a few seconds, then brakes suddenly and comes to an abrupt stop.

4

I CAN'T MEASURE THE TIME it takes us to get off the plane, reclaim our luggage and take a taxi. To me it's like a few minutes, rushing past like mice running from a flood.

I watch in dismay as the road speeds past the window. I wish the asphalt didn't look that way. Like the surface of a disc, a stream of grey lines without end. Maybe that's how it would seem to a racing driver if he was able to turn and look at it for a moment in the middle of a race, and yet according to the speedometer we aren't going fast at all, in fact we're going even slower than the permitted limit.

I keep telling myself it's just tiredness, I try to console myself with the thought that a comfortable suite awaits me at the hotel and I'll soon be sinking into a hot bath. The bellboy will be impeccable, as always, and as soon as he's wished me a good stay, this horrible feeling will immediately disappear.

We've arrived.

Again that thump in the chest. The journey only lasted a few minutes. I don't dare look at my watch, it was seven o'clock a moment ago, I have no desire to discover that it's already nine.

I give five little knocks on the door, lick my lips five times, count five steps and start again.

One, two, three, four, five.

One, two, three, four, five.

A way for me to catch my breath.

Federico and the others don't seem to be paying any attention to my difficulties, maybe they think I'm still trying to work off my fear of flying. He knows I don't like talking about my phobias, he'd never guess I'd actually like to be up there still, on that plane. *Still*, because it's not normal that we're already at the hotel.

With every step I take, I feel myself getting out of breath. I'd like to scream to everyone to stop. Slow down, why are you rushing like that? When did the porter take our luggage? And now where's he going so quickly? The concierge didn't even welcome us, he's like a broker spewing out numbers in the middle of the afternoon. The lift zooms up to the top floor, the doors open wide, am I the only one who feels as if they're throwing us out into the corridor? Before I set off towards my room I throw a last glance at Federico, my friend Federico, hoping he can see the panic in my eyes and decipher the messages I'm sending him. Try to help me, Fede, if you can.

"Go ahead, we'll catch you up," Federico says to the others, then takes me by the arm and draws me aside into a little sitting area off the corridor.

"Svevo, what's happening to you?"

I open my mouth to reply, but he interrupts me as if he's been waiting too long.

"Are you going to tell me what's happening? Don't you feel well? Is there anything we can do?"

I try to think up some explanation, but he's impatient. "If this is some kind of panic attack, I have tranquillizers."

"It's all right." I give up and let him walk me to the door of my room, letting him believe that the thought that I could take a tranquillizer if I wanted one has managed to relax me.

The room is as I expected to find it, which ought to reassure me: the blue carpet, an infinity of mirrors, everything perfect down to the smallest detail. Gaëlle and I will have a good time here tonight. I try to abandon myself to thoughts of that. The bed looks incredibly comfortable. I love pillows and there are as many as I want. It's still too early to get ready, so I can just collapse in the middle of these pillows and wait for everything to return to normal. Everything's under control, I keep telling myself, I'm just a bit tired.

There's a knock at the door. The porter must have forgotten an item of luggage.

I go to open it, and there's Federico, already dressed for the evening, staring at me with a puzzled look on his face.

"Haven't you changed yet? It's nearly ten. Gaëlle will be here any minute now. She said not to keep her waiting."

Again that thump in the chest. I run my hand through my hair.

"Are you tired? Did you fall asleep?"

How can I tell him I thought I'd only come into this room a few minutes ago? How can I explain that I wanted to take a bath more than anything else in the world and thought I had at least two hours to spare? There's no way, I can't even explain it to myself.

"Well, you might as well go like that. You don't look too bad, though you could comb your hair a bit... Are you sure you're feeling all right?"

Oh, yes, I'm all right. Yes, I'm perfectly all right. Apart from the fact that I have the impression I'm about to die at any moment. And apart from the fact that ever since I got on that damned plane my perception of time has turned upside down, I feel dirty and sweaty, and I have a premonition that I won't even have time to wash my hands. Maybe it's the drugs, Fede, we've taken too many of them over the past few years, there's no getting away from that, and now I'm paying for it, I'm paying the full price.

41

Or maybe this is the end, maybe I'm dying and before you die time goes faster to tell you that if there's anything you wanted to do in your life you'd better hurry up about it. But how can I tell you all this, my friend? Stop, at least give me time to try.

All at once I find myself in the car with Gaëlle, without having been able to do anything to prevent it. She's quite excited, happy to see me, and a wave of nausea takes me by the throat.

"Well, guys, how was the flight?" she asks, as she puts her foot down on the accelerator of her brand-new Mercedes.

I'd like to scream at her to let me out, but my mouth stays tightly shut.

"Everything was fine," Federico replies.

Gaëlle lightly touches my knee with one hand and looks at me hesitantly. "And you, darling? You look so pale."

All I can do is downplay the whole thing. "Everything's fine," I assure her.

She's wearing a draped black dress with a silver belt worn low on the waist, she looks like a Greek heroine, or rather a goddess, with her feet well planted on the ground in a pair of sandals with dizzyingly high heels. She's also wearing a weird little hat: a bouquet of feathers, like a coloured breath that has come to rest on her black hair, held in one of her most sophisticated hairdos. At any other time, I'd just have to look at her to regain my balance. Help me, Gaëlle, if your beauty can't do it, I really don't see what else can get me out of this nightmare.

"Everyone's there tonight, Svevo. You can't imagine the people who phoned me to ask for an invitation!"

I nod, feigning enthusiasm, and now we're already slowing down to look for a parking space.

The restaurant is packed, as usual. Everybody who matters in Paris is here, and many of them are desperate to say hello to us. And yet I feel like a goldfish in a bowl, with these people gawping at me through the glass like wide-eyed children. The world is all distorted, but I can't let this madness get the better of me, I can't allow it.

"*Alors, ça va, Svevo?*" It's Matthieu, a crazy painter in a gaudy striped jacket who probably thinks he's original. He calls himself the last of the abstract painters, he's actually just as much of an idiot as anyone else.

"You're here, too... *C'est magnifique!*"

And here's his muse, Charlotte, five foot three of femininity. On any other occasion I would have rattled off one of my usual compliments, but not tonight, tonight I don't feel like talking. Wherever I turn there's someone smiling, expecting something, a greeting, a joke. There are quite a few people here who might be useful to me in my business, but I can't say anything, I seem to have left all my enthusiasm on that plane.

I feel embalmed, the city is moving around me unaware of my anguish. Meanwhile, Matthieu is deafening me with his observations, which don't seem to follow any logical thread. Gaëlle has ordered for the two of us, and a second later she tells me my filet has already—*already*—arrived.

From the little I'm able to understand, I get the impression they're all talking rubbish. I must have involuntarily raised my eyes to heaven, because Gaëlle throws me a reproving look, she can't stand my impatience, tonight of all nights she really wants everything to be perfect.

As I eat I have the feeling my perception of time is going back to normal, but it's a false feeling, because when I look up from my plate, I realize that everybody has already finished, whereas I've barely touched my filet. To reassure everyone, Federico makes an ironic comment on how slow I am.

"Svevo, what's happening to you? Do you need someone to feed you?"

The table explodes in one of those laughs that echo, and I make an effort to smile, though what I'd really like to do is kill the lot of them.

Yet another panic attack. I don't know if I can control it this time, I'm being sucked into a vortex of anxiety. What's happening to me? What if it isn't time that's going faster but me who's slowed down? Do these people think I'm coming down from a bad trip? Who would take me seriously if I tried to explain what I'm experiencing? What if I really am coming down from a bad trip? The drugs last night. Maybe they were badly cut. Or maybe I've simply gone mad. Maybe that's the way it happens, suddenly, without anybody being able to do anything about it.

Absorbed by my paranoia, I still don't see You for what You are: not an abstract entity, but a living being, who has me by the balls. I'm champing at the bit, but You won't let go. Maybe You're trying to teach me a lesson and You won't stop until You've brought me to my knees.

"I'm fine, I don't want any more." I refuse to order a sweet. I pass, as if I'm playing poker, even though my stomach is twisted with cramp and I don't have an iota of energy left in my body.

"Shall we go?"

Gaëlle says this to Federico, not me. I guess she's alienated by the way I'm behaving and is intent on making me pay for it. And Federico plays along with her. If he wasn't my best friend, I'd have already given him a kick up the backside.

In the car I sit in the back, in order not to hinder their brilliant conversation. God, how I wish I was in Rome right now, independent, driving my baby, on my way home to do my own thing. But Gaëlle drives quickly, she's in a hurry to get to her party, she's hungry for adulation, she wants everyone clinging to her like insects to flypaper.

Forced smiles, laughing, overexcited faces. I can't stand anybody tonight. Their snobbish, cursory nodding, their longing to be admired. There they are, those four famous faces that come to life only under the spotlights, their thoughts on the people who'll be reading the gossip columns tomorrow, lingering over the most trivial details. The place is chaotic, people are pushing and shoving to get in through the doors. Reluctantly, they move aside to let us pass. On other occasions this triumphal entry would have amused me, especially on an evening when the flashbulbs are going off like crazy, but not tonight, I'm anxious and silent, I look like someone who's just survived a plane crash.

At a certain point I look at Gaëlle, who's going to want to sleep with me tonight, and panic takes hold of me again. I try to convince myself that my night with her won't just flash by, but will actually help me to find myself again.

"You look rough," she says, just inside the door. She's deliberately harsh, she wants to hurt me. She thinks she looks better than me, but I'm sober enough to notice her reddened nostrils, her slightly blackened teeth, her wild eyes circled in red. I don't have time to answer her, though, before she's already away, somewhere in the club, where all that matters is the music which everyone except me thinks is so infectious.

A friend of Gaëlle's I haven't seen in a while approaches me, says hello in an ingratiating tone, and immediately launches into a rapid monologue, the subject of which seems to be the boob job she had last week. Then she stops, presumably to give me time to say something, but I don't know for how long, the minutes flash past.

45

"*Tout va bien?*"

Her voice is so urgent, it's almost orgasmic.

"*Quelles nouvelles?*"

I'm about to make a superhuman effort to answer her, but luckily another orgasmic yelp tells me she's just caught sight of her next victim.

"Oh, Paul! So nice to see you! *Ça vaaa?*"

I lean over the balcony and look down. Two white marble staircases lead to the dance floor, where everyone's going wild to the feverish rhythm of unlistenable music. On a big block in the middle, two female dancers dressed as devils are jigging about, with pink feathers cascading down from the tops of their heads. At the far end of the room, mounted like a precious stone, is an impressive rocky fountain, on which a fire-eater is blowing flames over the heads of the crowd like an angry dragon. A club worthy of this city, and at any other time I might even have reflected on how thin and insubstantial the nightlife of Rome seems in comparison.

When I turn to say goodbye to Gaëlle's friend and leave her in the company of her new interlocutor, I realize that not only has she already sneaked away, but she's got as far as the fountain and is dancing next to the fire-eater.

I don't know if she told Paul about her boob job, but she must at least have said a few words to him, then gone down to the lower floor, made her way through the crowd to the fountain, jumped on one of the rocks and started to dance, all in what I perceived as a fraction of a minute at the most. I'm pretty sure she doesn't have superpowers.

I lean on the rail, I must look unsteady on my feet, I keep feeling I'm about to drown. I'm sweating, and my smell makes me feel nauseous, but so does everyone's smell. A fetid mixture of alcohol, smoke, heavy food and chewing gum. I have to get out of here.

I see Gaëlle dancing with Federico at the far end of the dance floor, next to the private area. Now she's getting up on the table they've reserved for us in the front row. Federico gives her a hand because she's had too much vodka and she could easily lose her balance. With her arse out and her head back, she's more provocative than usual. She needs to attract attention and she can do that better on a table. From up here they all seem so tiny, a colony of frenzied ants, and in the middle of them, there she is, Gaëlle, the queen. So proud of her little throne, a glass table, fragile and transparent.

I need to rinse my face with cold water. The toilets are behind me. Outside the Ladies, there's an interminable queue of mini-skirts and high heels.

Once in the toilet, I wipe my face with a handkerchief, then lean on the wall with a sigh. I start to feel a little bit better.

When I look up and peer into the semi-darkness of the wash-room, I make out the figure of a man who's just pinned a woman against the wall.

He's holding her wrists above her head to keep her still. She isn't putting up much of a struggle, her tapering fingers just seem a little slack. She's wearing a flashy-looking ring, like the one I gave Gaëlle last year. My Gaëlle.

She bends her long leg, letting him get in where nobody can see him. They sway back and forth a bit, slowly, and I notice that the woman has a silver belt, worn low on the waist, and metal sandals with dizzyingly high heels. Just like Gaëlle. My Gaëlle.

The man's hand moves down her bare thin arm, until it reaches her shoulder, and then again down, to her breasts. Against the

47

blood-red wall, I now see the bouquet of feathers the woman is wearing as a hat, just like Gaëlle. My Gaëlle.

I have a better view of the man now, too. Dark jeans, white shirt, curly, unkempt hair. Just like Federico. My friend Federico.

His bum sticking out, his feet splayed, his handmade leather moccasins. Again, just like Federico. My friend Federico.

I keep telling myself it can't be them, I saw them dancing in the private area downstairs only a moment ago. I flatten myself against the wall and creep towards the door, as if moving along a ledge. I'm dazed, I feel as if I've just been knocked on the head. At last I can hear what they're saying to each other.

"Don't be so impatient."

It's Gaëlle's voice, there's no mistaking it.

Knowing she's in a clinch with another man wipes me out. But what's even more disturbing is the thought that one second ago they were dancing on the other side of the club. They can't have flown here.

"Please, Federico, not now. Not with Svevo around."

"I beg you, I'm going crazy. Can't you see what you've done to me?"

Gaëlle smiles. A man who wants her, who'd do anything to have her, even betray his best friend: it's music to her ears.

"Just calm down now," she insists, affectionately, reassuringly. "I want you as much as you want me, but here and now it's crazy... You should have come without him, I told you. You knew this was going to happen..."

However unacceptable all this might be, I have no intention of walking away, or of intervening. I need to know.

"What would I have told Svevo? That I was going to Paris without him? To do what?"

"To be with me, if that isn't too ridiculous."

"Do you think I wouldn't like that, don't be absurd, it's just that I'm afraid he suspects… Ever since we arrived he's been very strange."

"It's impossible, trust me. Let me go, he could come in at any moment."

"You're killing me, don't you realize that?"

From Gaëlle's sighs, I deduce that they're rubbing themselves against each other again, and that Federico is at the stage when you start to lose control. Anger now gives way to pain.

"You're going to sleep with me tonight. That's not up for discussion." There's an authority in his voice I hardly recognize.

"I'll make up an excuse… Tell me your room number, and I'll come to you."

Now he's the one who's smiling. Just the thought of it makes him as excited as a little boy. There's no woman as good at exciting men as Gaëlle.

"I'm in Room 510, don't forget it. Five, like the happiest months of my life, the months I've known you. One, because I want to be the only man for you, and zero, because that's the number of seconds I'm prepared to wait."

Gaëlle laughs, and the sound echoes in my head like the laughter of witches in fairy stories when you're a child. I'd like to warn Federico, I'd like to tell him just how pathetic she is, and then kick him in the balls, so I leap forward and grab the doorpost with all the strength left in me, but when I thrust myself outside the toilet, there's nobody in the washroom. Gaëlle and Federico have vanished.

Again that feeling that my chest is in a vice, the ever more alarming sensation that I can't control what's happening. Time is crushing me like an insect. Maybe I'm the only ant in this crowd, the only one who doesn't know where he's going.

The entrance, where people were crowding in earlier, has suddenly emptied. The lights come on again, the music is over. Once again I refuse to look at my watch.

"Svevo!"

Gaëlle's voice surprises me. She's behind me.

"Where have you been?" Federico asks me as he helps her on with her coat. "We've been looking for you all evening. We thought you'd left."

How different it all seems now, the way they talk to me and look at each other.

"Where did you get to? Do you think it's right to behave the way you have?"

Gaëlle is in an argumentative mood, she's even more aggressive now than she was at dinner. She takes me aside. "Answer me, don't stand there like an idiot! Do you know it was Federico who paid the bill? I hope you'll pay him back. I don't understand you, you're a different person tonight. You should take a look in the mirror, you're behaving like a moron. Not to mention the way you made me look at dinner... I really don't know what's going through your head."

Her tone is unpleasant, to say the least. I look at her, and for the first time I'm indifferent to her beauty. I've never seen her looking so drawn, she doesn't even seem like the same person any more. She's a talking, moving shadow, a nasty thought that's best forgotten. Like the fear of time, of death, and of this night that's so fast and yet never seems to end.

I want to go back to the hotel, I don't care if she sleeps in the room next to mine or goes to bed with my best friend. I only want to get out of this hell.

Before getting in the car, I look Federico straight in the eyes. How dare he smile at me? But when I hear him ask me yet again, in that apprehensive, suspicious tone of his, if I'm sure I'm feeling all right, I realize I'm completely indifferent. Let him fuck her, I don't care. "You'd tell me, wouldn't you, if something was really wrong?" He comes even closer, as if he's about to rugby-tackle me, I think he's asking me to confirm his suspicions.

"Of course I'd tell you, I'm much better now. What about you, though?" I give him a sidelong glance. "What's the matter? You look tired. I imagine you can't wait to get back to the hotel, can you?"

He can't sustain my gaze any more, he doesn't have the balls. But I don't say anything more.

Gaëlle is more irritable than ever. "Well? Are we going?"

In this final lightning ride, all I have time to do is ruin the rest of the night for her. "Gaëlle, I'm tired. I hope you don't mind if we see you home, then take the car."

"Svevo, what's got into you tonight?"

I know her, she's on the verge of a scene.

"I'm sorry, I have a bad headache."

This certainly wasn't how she'd imagined our farewell. She was expecting to complain of a headache when we got to the door of my room, and to say something like, "Don't worry, it's all right, I'll call a taxi." Instead of which, I'm saying loud and clear that I don't want her tonight. She wasn't expecting anything as outrageous as that.

"Svevo, I swear I don't understand you! Do you want to take me home? Do you want my car? What is it you want?"

She's making an effort to keep calm.

"I've just explained, I'm very tired and I'd like to sleep alone. Let's not make a big song and dance about it, we'll see you home and for the sake of convenience we'll keep the car. Tomorrow morning I'll come and pick you up as soon as I'm awake."

She doesn't reply. I know her, she's angry and she feels humiliated by the thoughtless way I'm treating her. Even supposing she did decide to come back to our hotel, I think I've taken away any desire she may have had to sleep with another man. What was that ridiculous business with the room numbers? I'd like to see you knock at his door now, Gaëlle, in the mood you're in. When a woman like her is rejected, she can't just shrug it off straight away. I'm not exactly consoled by this, but it was all I could do. When we pull up outside her building, her dismayed expression as she watches us drive away and the image of Federico angrily pressing his foot on the accelerator have a liberating effect on me, and for a moment all my anguish seems to fade.

Once I'm alone in my room, though, it comes back, more insistent than ever, and won't leave me in peace. I take off my shirt and shoes, then collapse on the bed still wearing my jeans. I try to let my head sink into the pillow, but now that there are no more voices and noises around me, the thoughts come rushing into my mind. All I can do is start counting again: those five words I still have a little trust in.

One, two—

I'm interrupted by a loud knock at the door that makes me jump. Then another one, and yet another, like a violent hammering on my temples.

"Svevo, it's Federico!"

What does he want at this hour of the night? I don't have time for belated confessions or requests for forgiveness, I only want to try and relax.

"What's the matter, Federico?"

The door is flung open and daylight floods the room.

Federico is standing there in front of me, washed and dressed and rested. Once again he stares at me, he wasn't expecting to find me like this, a soaking wet rag drenched in tiredness.

"I've been knocking at your door for ages," he says. "I was about to call the bellboy. I came to tell you we're ready to go to lunch."

It's day. The light proves it.

I'm mad. The light proves it.

5

TWO NIGHTMARISH DAYS have passed. Paris, my Paris, the most beautiful city in the world, with all its elegant buildings, suffocated me. All I ever did there was run. Run to dinner, run for coffee, run to talk to people and pretend to be cheerful and relaxed, even when I was making an effort to look at Gaëlle and Federico as if they were still my friends.

Maybe I'm at the peak of a particularly stressful period. Whatever it is, my life just isn't the same any more, I've been flung into a new dimension, a reality where there only seem to be half the number of hours in the day as there were before, where, if I'm lucky, I have to be content with sleeping two or three hours a night, and my appointments and deadlines are so close together I can't handle them.

It should be seven o'clock on Monday morning, and I'm in bed, clinging to the last moments of sleep, knowing the alarm clock will go off very soon.

Instead of which, it's the entryphone that buzzes, insistently, as if saying, "Hurry up, Svevo, hurry up!"

I leap out of bed and stagger to the door, my eyes still half-closed. I'd turned off the heating before leaving for Paris, and this morning it's freezing cold, the parquet floor seems like a sheet of ice, and with every step I take a shiver runs down my spine.

"Who is it?"

"It's the doorman, Signor Romano. The driver's here asking if you need him."

"Of course I need him. What the hell is the time?"

"It's ten past nine. We were wondering if everything was all right."

I'm almost used by now to the pain I feel in my chest every time I'm told the time.

I've started to imagine You. I've given You human form, because I need a face to direct my anger at. I think of You as busy keeping things moving, making sure nothing ever stops. Father Time and his everlasting work. You've decided to make me skip a few stages, You've suddenly gone all frantic, full of fits and starts. What are You trying to do? Declare war on me? I have to tell You, I'm not someone who gives up easily. I won't submit to this madness, I won't screw up the things I've built up with so much effort over the past few years, even if I have to do without sleep, food or sex. I have no intention of throwing in the towel.

I'm outside the building in half an hour, real time, which in my time is only fifteen minutes, more or less. Antonio is waiting for me at the wheel, surprised that I kept him waiting so long and that I'm in such a tearing hurry now. I have to control myself, the situation is critical, but I can do it, I keep telling myself.

My diary is chock-a-block with appointments I can't afford to miss. I have to keep everything in order, I mustn't get all the documents mixed up. I have to run, yes, but I have to do it intelligently. I have to be faster than You, I tell myself, but at the same time try to keep control. During the ride I count to five—one, two, three, four, five, one, two, three, four, five—never taking my eyes off the street, because if I get distracted, You'll swallow the ride. But then I take a second glance at my diary and when I look up I see Antonio looking at me uneasily, wondering why I'm waiting to get out of the car. We've already pulled up outside the office and according to my watch it's 10.30.

Once inside, too, I'm greeted by puzzled faces. Starting with Paola, the switchboard operator, whom in my hurry I barely acknowledge. Running to my office, I almost collide with Elena and all her papers.

"Good morning," she says, with a sigh.

"I'm sorry... Good morning, Elena," I reply, breathlessly.

"Did you forget?"

"What?"

"That you had an appointment with Righini at nine this morning. We tried to call you, but your phone was off."

I take it out of my pocket and realize I haven't recharged it. I haven't had time.

"Shit!" I cry, which isn't my style at all. How could I have forgotten? Then I try to regain my composure. "I guess the director's been looking for me, too."

"Yes, I had to tell him that Righini was waiting for you, and he asked me to take him to his office."

"Has he already left?"

"They talked for about an hour, no more than that. Then they stopped waiting for you, I don't know if they rescheduled the meeting."

I grab my papers, trying not just to stuff them in my briefcase, then leave my office and rush to the director's office as quickly as I can.

Things are at a delicate stage, the director warned me not to miss that appointment. It was a false move, and it's unforgivable. I hope it isn't the first in a long series.

SIMONA SPARACO

"Good morning, Caterina," I stammer to the director's secretary. "Can you tell him I'm here?"

"Of course, Signor Romano."

She opens the door and motions me to go in.

"Please, sit down."

I feel the blood freeze in my veins, I haven't yet thought of a plausible excuse for my behaviour.

"Romano, Romano… I can't believe what happened this morning! Not even a phone call to warn me…"

That's how he begins as he comes towards me, breathing hard, his voice booming. Then he stops and just stands there, looking at me solemnly.

He isn't tall, but with his bullet-like head and sparse, well-groomed grey hair, he conveys a powerful sense of authority and always carries himself like someone who expects to be treated with the greatest deference. "I'm not interested in your excuses," he says, although I haven't even had time to breathe. "Do we at least have a draft contract?"

"I have it with me," I try to say, but he silences me with a stern look.

"You know how important this acquisition is for us. We could probably have closed the deal today. You know as well as I do, time is money."

"You're right, I have no excuse."

By the time he sits down at his desk he's calmed down a bit. He looks at me again, almost regretfully, but I don't think I've really disappointed him, because he assumes there are valid reasons for my behaviour. Except that he's not interested in hearing them. "Time is money, old friend," he repeats.

"I know, I know that better than you think."

He opens the silver box where he keeps his cigars, and takes

58

one out. "The one unfailing duty we have to ourselves, Svevo, is never to forget who we are and where we're going."

All at once, from behind a cloud of smoke, he calls his secretary and orders her to come and take away a glass. It's a crystal glass, perfectly clean, but he sees a smudge on it and it bothers him. He instructs Caterina to check them carefully, one by one, nobody must be allowed to use his glasses. When Caterina leaves the room, he takes a disinfectant wipe from his drawer, rubs his hands with it and says, "You can go now. Keep me up to date with developments. Remember I gave you this assignment, knowing how delicate it was, and I don't like regretting the decisions I make."

Once I'm out in the corridor, I'm tormented by a new anxiety: what if I've lost his trust? I wouldn't like to be forced to hand in my resignation before the end of the year.

"I'm going to lunch, Signor Romano," Elena tells me when I get back to my office. "I left a list of telephone numbers on your desk, it's been impossible to get hold of you today."

"What do you mean, lunch? What time is it?"

"1.30. Do you mind if I go now?"

I think I must have turned pale, because Elena continues to stare at me questioningly.

"No... no, I don't mind," I say, making an effort to seem convincing. "I'll see you in half an hour, not a minute more, we have a lot to do this afternoon."

Elena walks away, deeply puzzled. I think she's guessed that something isn't right, all this urgency isn't like me, but there's no way she can imagine the kind of absurdity that has me in its grip, or how much I need her on my side.

"Oh, I forgot," she says as she's about to leave the room. "Your father phoned, it sounded important."

That's the last thing I need right now. "If he calls again, tell him I don't have time."

When I sit down at the desk, the running starts again. The desk is overflowing with sheets, documents, deadlines, I have to check my calls, the appointments I've missed, and as if that wasn't enough my mobile phone doesn't stop ringing. I need to exploit every minute, even invent others if necessary, but I have to get back on the rails as soon as possible.

If there's one thing I'm not good at, it's apologizing. Especially when I've kept Engineer Baldi, a well-known entrepreneur, waiting for twenty minutes in the café of a hotel. It's hardly surprising that he goes off the deep end when I phone him. As he's giving me a dressing down, I check my e-mails. If I don't want to be overtaken by events, I have to learn to do two or three things at the same time.

We fix another appointment for tomorrow morning at nine. "Don't mess me about," Baldi says threateningly before hanging up. And as if that wasn't enough, almost simultaneously, a text message comes from Federico: *What are we doing tonight?*

I don't have time for his bullshit, not even to tell him to fuck off, which is what I ought to do. I'm in a car that's travelling at three hundred kilometres an hour, I can't allow myself any distraction, if I even just touch the wheel distractedly the race will be over. It's pointless to mull over the past, or the feeling of disappointment it's left me with, the bitter taste that's gradually fading. Right now I have more important things to think about.

"Signor Romano, Righini on the phone."

It's Elena on speakerphone.

"You were quick."

"I'm really sorry I was late, but it isn't easy to eat in less than half an hour."

My God, I'd meant it as a joke, and it wasn't.

"Put him through, thanks. Righini, hello."

"Hello, Romano, you pulled a nasty stunt on me this morning."

"I tried to call you earlier to apologize. I'm really, really sorry."

"I know, your secretary updated me. Unfortunately I don't have much time now, I'm in the middle of a working lunch. I just called to tell you I'm leaving for Hong Kong on Thursday and I'll be there for about three weeks, I think I told you, didn't I?"

"Yes, of course… But weren't you supposed to leave about the end of the month?"

"I had to bring it forward."

"So I suppose fixing another meeting in three days' time is out of the question?"

"Unfortunately, yes. I couldn't tell your director about it this morning, because I only heard about it at midday myself. As soon as I get back I'll be sure to phone you."

"In that case, all I can do is wish you a safe journey."

"Thank you, we'll speak when I get back."

I shouldn't have missed that appointment this morning, it's obvious Righini is only trying to gain time, maybe he's rethinking the conditions of the sale, maybe he's under pressure from another buyer. The deal might go belly up, and all because of what? Because one morning I opened my eyes and before I could even get out of bed an hour had already passed. Now the problem will be to tell the director. Shit, shit, shit.

"Try to find out what's going on," the director tells me. "Do some research, talk to people, and pray to the Lord that Righini doesn't have second thoughts."

61

His message is unambiguous: the consequences of this mess are all on my shoulders.

"Signor Romano?"

Elena has put her head in through the door.

"Yes?"

"Is it all right if I go?"

"Where?"

"What do you mean, where?" Her eyes open wide in surprise. "It's nearly eight, we always go home now. Usually even earlier when you go to the gym. Not going today? Tired after your weekend?"

I'm more scared than I was this morning. You don't get used to a thing like this.

No gym, no lunch, no phone calls or any of the many other things I should have done. I have to go home and get something in my belly as soon as possible.

I've never before skipped gym on a Monday, or got back earlier than nine. Antonio hasn't asked any questions, but I know he doesn't like sudden changes in the programme, and we're going to end up paying him a fortune in overtime. I only hope this condition isn't degenerative and that tomorrow won't be worse than today.

I get back very late. I drop my things on the sofa and glance at the dinner my housekeeper always leaves me on the kitchen table. Usually it's warm, tonight it's cold.

I stick it in the microwave and set the timer for one minute, keeping my eyes fixed on the control panel.

There it is, that minute, one second after the other. This way it won't escape me. The trick is not to be distracted, you just have to turn your head for a moment and the clock runs ahead. That means I have to live without ever taking my eyes off a watch or clock of some kind. It doesn't strike me as a very reasonable solution.

Instead of relaxing on the sofa, as I would have done any other evening I spent at home, I try to get ahead of myself, organizing my diary, setting the alarm on my mobile phone for my nine o'clock appointment with Baldi—making sure I increase the volume so that I don't miss its ringing—preparing my papers, getting my clothes ready for tomorrow. Finally, I collapse onto the bed without even looking at my watch. There's no point knowing how much time I have left to sleep, I just have to sleep and that's it.

6

A N INTERMITTENT WHISTLING SOUND. Five seconds, then silence for another ten, and so on, three or four times in succession. In my sleep, it becomes the whistle of a train about to depart.

In my dream I'm standing on a platform. The station is ultra-modern, but the train in front of me is a nineteenth-century one, impatiently belching steam. I'm waiting for Gaëlle, she's supposed to be bringing me my luggage, but she's taking too long and the ticket inspector is gesturing to me to hurry up.

The loudspeaker announces the departure, and people rush past me, anxious to get seats. I stand there motionless, waiting for her, but inside I can feel myself exploding with anger.

All at once, I see her emerge from among the crowd and run towards me. She's wearing a tight-fitting bright-red tracksuit, like the ones those devils wore in the club in Paris. Her hair blows in the wind, and she's more beautiful than ever, but there's no sign of my case. She looks at me with her usual wicked smile, then slows down, and when we're just a short distance from each other she says, "Svevo, you don't have anything to take with you and you can't leave like this. Stay with me, when it comes down to it you're not capable of going anywhere."

"What are you saying, Gaëlle? The train's about to leave."

"I see that. But without you."

"Give me my case."

"That's not the problem."

Another whistle.

"Give me my case!"

"There is no case, Svevo. There was nothing in your case."

Yet another whistle, this time more insistent.

"Stop it, Gaëlle! Bring me my case!" I continue to shout until, groping between the sheets, I realize the whistle is the buzzing of the entryphone, the doorman must be pressing the button again and again.

I drag myself to the door, my eyes still gummy with sleep. "Who is it?"

"Antonio's here, waiting for you, Signor Romano. Is everything all right? Do you need any help?"

Apparently I didn't hear the alarm clock today either.

"What time is it?"

"A quarter past nine."

Shit! The appointment with Baldi.

"I'll be down in a quarter of an hour, tell him to wait."

If I was able to get dressed in five minutes, I'd get to the front door in a fraction of real time, but that doesn't take unexpected factors into account, like the fact that they forgot to close the lift door and as I'm running down the stairs my briefcase opens and a myriad of papers spills onto the steps. Then in the hall I knock straight into the doorman's wife, who's cleaning the floor, and she ends up practically in my arms. More time wasted apologizing and saying goodbye.

At last I get to the car. Impatiently, I order Antonio to drive as fast as he can, and he obeys, with the same grimace of disgust he had last night. I'm indecently late, and I'm trying to find an excuse to give Baldi, but I barely have time to go through all the possible justifications, because we've already arrived at the hotel. Baldi is on his second espresso, and he's crimson with rage.

"I really don't know how to apologize."

"Another minute and I'd have gone."

"I'm sorry."

"Do you think you can just keep people waiting like this?"

"Please forget this unfortunate incident."

"And the one yesterday? Should I forget yesterday's incident, too?"

A moment's silence, then, fortunately, his face again takes on a more natural colour, and a more indulgent expression. He signals to the waiter. "Let's get down to business," he says. "I have a lot of work to get on with this afternoon."

"Of course," I reply, taking out the papers. "In the meantime can I offer you something to drink?"

"Another espresso would do me fine."

"Good. Two espressos please, and make mine a double."

Baldi immediately gets to the point, but I have difficulty following him. I don't seem to be able to concentrate any more, my mind seems to be elsewhere. I'm sure the things he's saying—the figures, the names, the projections—are perfectly clear and logical, he's a highly competent businessman after all, and yet more than once I ask him to repeat what he just said. Trying to stay calm, he does as I ask. I discover that if I keep my eyes firmly on my watch it's easier to follow what he's saying, but eventually he loses patience. "Do you want me to explain it again? Do you think I'm wasting your time? Do you think your behaviour is acceptable?" Now he's the one glancing at his watch. "I have to go," he says irritably. "Have your director call me."

It hits below the belt, but in his place I'd have done the same. He says goodbye coldly and goes.

No sooner have I switched my mobile on again than it starts ringing.

It's Elena. "It's nearly midday," she says. "Signora Campi is waiting for you in the meeting, don't you remember?"

I feel a sharp pain in my spleen, and my face twists into a grimace. The waiter is looking at me. "Are you all right?"

I leave the money on the table and run away.

Barbara Campi is waiting for me in the doorway of the conference room with her arms crossed. "Six people from the marketing department have been waiting for you for an hour and a half."

"I'm sorry..." That seems to be the only thing I can say today.

She raises her eyebrows, then gives a sardonic sneer. No, I'm not mistaken, it really is a sneer. It's almost as if she's saying, "You see, you male chauvinist, you're not so infallible. And you still have the nerve to attack us for our miniskirts, our laddered stockings, and the children always waiting for us to pick them up from school."

I rub my face with my hands, I must look terrible.

"Do you have any idea of the time you've made us waste?"

"Believe me," I reply with a bitter smile, "nobody knows that more than I do."

She stares at me. "Are you kidding me?" she says. "You never even answered my e-mail, I have to know what you think about the plans for the new promotional campaign..."

I have no intention of putting up with another incomprehensible monologue. "Barbara, please..."

Her eyes open wide. I can't bear that expression of hers, she's like the class swot, if we were at school she'd raise her hand to tell the teacher I'd made lots of mistakes. "Are you feeling all right? I just found out you missed the appointment with Righini. God knows when you'll be able to see him again. You look distracted, I'm worried about you."

I've always had the feeling that when somebody's worried about you, it's more a matter of form, or even of self-interest, than because they really care. That's definitely the case with Barbara. The health of one of the company's executives is certainly not high on her list of priorities, especially when the executive in question is a cynical, selfish bachelor, and not exactly a friend of hers.

"I'm just tired. It happens to all of us sometimes, doesn't it?"

"Of course it happens," she says in a reassuring voice, but with a hypocritical gleam in her eyes. Then she smiles, and advises me to look after myself. "And don't get too thin. You know, don't you, that eighty per cent of the women in this office think you're some kind of Greek god?"

"And are you in that eighty per cent?"

She smiles again. "No, I'm in the hundred per cent that basically hates you."

Beaming with amusement, she walks away along the corridor. A moment later, Elena joins me.

"I just can't keep up with you today," she says, and I assume that having constantly to follow me around is starting to get on her nerves. "You were supposed to be having lunch with the director and Deputy Incerti."

"Yes, I know. Why? What time is it?"

"2.30," she says, shrugging her shoulders and shaking her head. "I got back from my lunch hour and came to find you. You left your mobile in your office."

Barbara again appears in the corridor. "You haven't eaten either," I say to her, trying to conceal my dismay, but she smiles, taking my statement as a joke.

"Actually, I had a big plate of noodles. What about you? Didn't you go with the director? I told you only an hour ago, make sure you don't get too thin."

7

I NEVER KNEW this condition existed, I never knew there was a mental disorder that could catapult a person into a reality like this. Somehow I've managed to get through a month of this, and I'm still alive. And I still don't consider myself completely mad, schizophrenic or a would-be suicide.

In these thirty long and very short days, I've avoided any kind of serious conversation, I haven't been to the gym or gone out in the evening. At weekends I've shut myself up in my apartment to recover all the hours of sleep I'd lost during the week, though I have the feeling that doing nothing only makes time go even faster. I ignore the phone calls from friends. The only stable relationship I have is with the message service of my mobile phone. I've never talked so much to anyone in all my life, although all I do is record trivial things to remind myself that I have to remember them. I'm struggling to keep my head above water, to save face and my career, but today I really think I touched bottom, and if I don't make an effort to come back up I'll soon be forced to ask for help.

It was about lunchtime and I was in my office, I felt as if I was suffocating, the air was becoming unbreathable. After a while, I started to lose concentration, my eyes were smarting with tiredness. Elena kept throwing me sympathetic glances, as if to say, "Go home, please, I can't bear to see you in this state." Over the past month, everybody at work has started looking at me the same way. And the director is unrecognizable, he's like someone in mourning: from a work point of view, I'm the equivalent of a son to him.

I decided to follow Elena's tacit advice, I said goodbye to those I needed to say goodbye to and left, switching off my mobile. I asked Antonio to take me to the gym. He seemed happy to know that at least for one evening he'd get back home and see his wife earlier than he'd thought.

I wasn't in the mood to start lifting weights, all I wanted was a massage from Donatella, my favourite therapist, and a quick sauna.

"Where have you been keeping yourself, Svevo?" she asked, greeting me with one of her big smiles.

"I've been working too hard, I need one of your massages to feel human again."

She kept smiling at me all the way to her room. Once inside, I tried to undress as quickly as possible, she switched off the light slightly impatiently and then whispered excitedly in my ear, "At last, Svevo. I was afraid you wouldn't come any more."

I touched her lips with my finger and begged her to give me the kind of massage that makes you lose all sense of time.

She nodded, and started with my feet, as sensually as ever. Little undulating circles, which in less than no time reached my buttocks, where she lingered only for a few seconds, before climbing gently, but quickly, to my shoulders.

I'd hoped, in closing my eyes, that at least this massage would last long enough to relax me, but after not even twenty minutes—of my time—Donatella had already finished.

"How about a nice Turkish bath?" she whispered in her friend-liest Roman accent.

She's beautiful, Mediterranean, sensuality personified. A pity about her heavy make-up, which makes her look vulgar, and about that black ponytail that's pulled back so tightly it makes her look as if she's had a facelift. I've only slept with her a couple of times, and in normal circumstances would gladly have repeated the experience now.

She kissed me on the lips. "If I could, I'd keep you company," she said, putting her ointments away.

With an instinctive gesture I grabbed her by the ponytail and kissed her roughly. She pulled back. "I can't, I'm at work. Why don't you invite me over for a little supper sometime? I've almost forgotten where you live."

I noticed I was getting an erection. It was a relief to know I still could.

"What do you say, Svevo? How about the day after tomorrow?"

"Nine o'clock."

"Don't stand me up…"

"I'm not that mad."

Then she walked me to the Turkish bath, arranged the towels next to the washbasin and said goodbye. "You know what you have to do. Ten minutes, then take a cold shower, and if you want to, repeat three or four times. See you the day after tomorrow, darling!"

So I made my way through the steam and lay down on one of the marble steps. As soon as the heat enveloped me, I started to feel pleasantly relaxed.

Immediately afterwards I lost consciousness.

When I came to, three or four pairs of eyes were looking anxiously at me. My legs were being lifted in the air by the secretary, Donatella was pressing a cold cloth on my forehead and the bodybuilding instructor was ordering a young boy to bring some water and sugar.

"How do you feel? Donatella asked, anxiously.

"Fine, what happened?"

"You collapsed," the instructor said, with a frown. "It's lucky we noticed in time. You spent fifty minutes inside a Turkish bath… It could have killed you."

Fifty minutes. My heart started pounding. I had to get dressed and go home.

Fifty minutes. I kept thinking about the tragedy I'd narrowly avoided, at the same time as insisting that I wanted to go and assuring everybody that I felt better. "Are you sure you feel all right?" Donatella asked, still pestering me with her cold cloth.

"Perfectly all right." A few minutes more and I'd have died in the corner of a Turkish bath. And all because fifty minutes for my body no longer correspond to fifty minutes in my mind. What a stupid end.

I got home at ten, but for once You weren't what was uppermost in my thoughts. I have the impression I'm doomed to remain motionless, like a disenchanted spectator, while my life is going downhill and no one can do anything to stop it. When the spotlights are turned off, darkness will invade everything. The mere thought of the negation of ourselves is chilling.

First, an infinity of emotions, life in all its overwhelming intensity, then suddenly nothingness. A body huddled in a corner, hidden by the steam of a Turkish bath, and someone picking it up, almost with horror, and stuffing it in a big plastic bag like any other piece of rubbish. The end of everything. And not even knowing how the people who gather for your funeral will behave. The fear that nobody might be experiencing genuine grief, nobody will have the feeling as they make their way home that part of them has died along with you, that nobody will think you're irreplaceable. And it can happen just like that, in an instant. You look around and thirty years are nothing but a handful of memories, and the other thirty to come, even assuming there are thirty, look set to go by even faster. Tomorrow, I could wake up already old. I wonder if my last thought will be of You. Deep down there's only oblivion, and it's never before seemed so overwhelming to me. It's poked its head out, and however absurd it may seem, nobody can hope to escape it.

Drring, drring.

It's the penetrating ring of my new alarm clock, the one I bought when I realized I couldn't keep letting the doorman wake me.

It's 6.30, and my race is about to start.

My meeting with Righini, who's just got back from Hong Kong, has been fixed for midday, so I can at least find a few seconds to devote to the mirror.

It turns out not to be such a good idea. I look like a mess, my face is pale and emaciated. I must have lost a few kilos, which doesn't cheer me up at all.

As I comb my hair, I think again about my Aston Martin, I haven't seen her since before Paris and I'm starting to miss her. She represents everything my life was until not so long ago: an unconscious race. Always a few friends or a pretty woman on board, me throwing the keys to a valet outside some exclusive club or other, a crowd of people stopping to watch us. It's in homage to these memories that I decide I'll steal a few seconds today to drop by the garage and say hello to my baby.

The garage is dark, especially early in the morning when the shutters haven't been completely raised and the light gives out before it gets to the far end. I step carefully, searching for her among the many parked cars, and my mounting sense of expectation makes me want to take her away, to go for a ride in her.

There she is, a black shadow calling to me through the air damp with the smell of tyres and fuel. I keep walking, admiring her from a distance, but then stop abruptly when I realize that where my baby should be there's nothing but a heap of dusty scrap metal.

There must be some mistake.

No mistake, that's my number plate.

What the hell kind of joke is this? I feel faint. I take a step forward, then another one, five very slow steps that take me into her decaying presence.

Not even a fire or an act of vandalism could have reduced her to that state. She seems to have aged a thousand years, as if she'd been abandoned in some remote part of the world. She's in pieces, completely covered in dust, her wheels askew, her bodywork dented, her leather interior torn to shreds: who could have done something like this?

"Stefano!"

The garage owner comes out of his lodge, almost scared. "Signor Romano, what is it?"

"My Aston Martin! What the hell happened to her?"

Stefano turns pale. "Nothing, Signor Romano, absolutely nothing."

Like hell, nothing. "Come and see!"

We hurry through the garage, me in a panic and Stefano worried about an incident he can't even explain.

"Who touched her?" I scream at him. "Who the hell touched her? She's a collector's item, don't you realize that?"

"Signor Romano, please, let me just see... I don't understand."

There she is. There at the far end. Her silhouette stands out against the white wall, in the almost luminescent darkness. She looks newer than ever. Not a scratch, not even a speck of dust.

I'm as embarrassed as he is, although he heaves a sigh of relief and looks at me in a daze.

"I'm really sorry," I stammer. "It's just that... I don't know... I can't have looked properly. It was all... Let's just forget it, I'm sorry."

He doesn't know what to say. He goes to the car and takes a closer look at her. "Do you want me to keep her covered with a sheet?"

She's perfect. He walks round her twice, then stops.

"What exactly did you see?"

"I must have made a mistake."

"Can I go now?" he asks, discomfort in his eyes.

"Yes, go. And again, I'm sorry."

The situation is getting worse.

The shock has drained me of all energy. I open the car door and collapse into the perfectly intact seat. I hunch over the wheel, my hands sweating. I caress it as I used to do, almost as if saying hello to it. I let out a first, impatient sob. There's no point holding it back, because others will come, they're lining up in my throat, ready to come out, one by one, without my being able to do anything to stop them.

When I look up, between my tears I see a figure watching me from a distance. I try to bring it into focus.

The figure sways towards me, until I recognize the curly beard.

"Signor Romano? Are you all right?" It's the voice of Antonio, my driver.

I feel as if he's just caught me stealing or doing something unmistakably obscene. I quickly wipe my tears and try to regain my composure. "Yes, I'm fine."

"Are you sure?"

Now I feel like laughing. "No, I'm not," I say with a bitter sneer. "But who can say they're really fine?"

"Do you want me to call a doctor?"

"There's no point."

"Do you want to talk to someone?"

"The two of us have never before said anything except good morning, the name of a street and goodbye," I say, curling my lips in regret.

Antonio listens to me without understanding. "Is there anything I can do for you?" he asks, a tad embarrassed.

"There's no one who can really help me. Just tell me what time it is."

"It's lunchtime," he tells me, handing me my mobile phone. "Your secretary called several times. I didn't want to disturb you, so I took the liberty of answering. She seemed very agitated. Apparently you had an appointment with somebody called Righini? What should I do? Take you back to the office?"

It's the end. What a stupid fucking end.

8

THE DIRECTOR comes into my office, so furious that Elena sneaks away in fright. He slams the door behind him, then turns to look at me, and for a few moments he stands there, completely silent.

Then he explodes.

"Have you gone completely mad?"

"I'm really sorry," I stammer, "there was an accident."

"Is missing two appointments in a row with the major share-holder of Benefil what you call an accident? Unless you ended up in the morgue, I don't accept any excuses."

His eyes are overflowing with contempt.

"It'll never happen again," I promise. No sooner are the words out than I regret them.

"You're making me lose patience, Romano! You have no idea of the embarrassment you caused us this morning. Do you know what Righini said before he left, after waiting three quarters of an hour?"

I keep quiet.

"Of course you don't, because while Righini was slamming the door in our faces you were fast asleep! And you didn't even deign to answer your mobile!"

He manages to make me feel really inept.

"You're completely unreliable," he continues, his tone calmer now, almost detached. "Look at yourself, your shirt's always creased, your tie's twisted, you haven't shaved. Not so long ago, you were famous for your sharp, intelligent answers, now you never seem to know what to say. Those rambling speeches and long pauses are becoming unbearable. You aren't even the shadow of the young man I knew a few years ago."

Those rambling speeches and long pauses. So that's how I seem to people: slow, lost, adrift.

The director begins silently pacing the room, casting a clinical eye on even the most insignificant of details. My desk has never been so untidy, I have no idea how many files and magazines have piled up over the past few days, my coat hangs indolently over the armchair, and my briefcase is open, its contents spilling onto the floor.

"Aren't you feeling well?" he asks me. "At least tell me if something serious has happened to you." It's paradoxical that the only thing that could make him feel less anxious would be if I was sick.

I don't know what to say. For the first time in his presence, I want to bow my head, like a pupil who hasn't done his homework confronted by an impatient teacher.

"You don't have a family," he continues, "a wife, children. I can only assume it's a health problem. Is someone not well? Give me an acceptable explanation, Svevo, you owe it to me, I wouldn't like to be forced to take action."

I still don't have any answer for him. He's very insistent, and I don't have enough time. In the end I decide to take the easy way out. "I'm fine," I assure him. "I'm just going through a difficult time. I can't really talk about it, just give me the chance to put things right."

"You're mixing your private and professional lives, Romano," he says, a hint of impatience in his voice. "And now you want to put things right. For more than a month you've been haunting this office like a ghost. Always late, tired, distracted, negligent. You're gradually losing the respect and trust of the people who work with you."

I imagine Barbara, with her thin lips and pinched nostrils, saying to him, "He doesn't fit in with our plans, sir. Get rid of him."

"There are some things that can't be put right," he goes on. "That's the way the world is, take it or leave it. You're young, you're good, you still have time to change your ways."

The director picks up my coat disdainfully with his fingertips and hangs it on the rack. I'm transfixed, watching him as he rubs his hand with the usual disinfectant wipe. Then he lights a cigar, sits down in the armchair, and, with his mouth full of smoke, orders me to take a holiday.

I try to reply, but he doesn't give me time.

"Maybe I didn't make myself clear, it wasn't advice. I don't want to see you in this office for at least a week. You put me in a difficult position with Righini this morning. I can't let you cause me any more problems."

I bow my head, to show how contrite I am.

"Listen to me," he says, in a more conciliatory tone. "Take that holiday, and the old Romano will soon be back in action. Don't forget the eohippus. You don't want to end up like the pterodactyl, do you?"

I still can't believe he hasn't thrown me out on my ear. I was expecting a firing squad, instead of which he's been almost too lenient.

I'm alone again. Elena puts her heads in round the door. "May I?"

"Of course, Elena, what is it?"

She advances uncertainly to the desk, her anxiety clear in every gesture. "I'd like to apologize for this morning," she says.

"What do you mean?"

"I'm your secretary. When you left the office yesterday, I should have reminded you of the appointment."

I give her an affectionate smile. "It's not your fault."

Elena nods. Only now do I realize that her watch, unlike mine, is still five minutes ahead. A sense of inadequacy overcomes me. As she's about to leave the room, I ask her to stop for another moment.

"Should I sit down?"

"Sit in the armchair, I need to talk to you."

She seems hesitant, she doesn't know where to look, but I know that by this point nothing could surprise her any more, and I need to clarify things, to talk to somebody.

"I feel like someone who doesn't have time on his side," I confess to her, after a long sigh. "But you must have guessed that by now, it's never pursued me the way it has lately."

This kind of confidence makes her feel uncomfortable. "It's not a problem," she says quickly, "it's my job."

"No. It's never been your job to pick up after me when I miss meetings and lunches. And I want to thank you for doing it. You've always organized my life efficiently and it's not your fault I've gone off the rails."

Her face relaxes, and she smiles at me.

"I'm going through a strange phase," I continue. "I'm finding even the simplest things really difficult. You're trying to limit the damage and I'd like you to continue doing that."

"Of course. You don't even have to ask. I'm sorry you're having problems and I hope you manage to solve them."

"Everything passes in the end, Elena. This'll pass, too."

I fall silent and she glances at her watch. I know I'm taking up much more of her time than I think I am. I tell her she can go.

"Don't worry," she says encouragingly as she gets to the door, "you know you can count on me."

Once she's gone, I turn to look at the window.

What I see is a grim view of a city driven mad by the frenzied pace of its inhabitants. A poisonous curtain of smog lies over the streets, the parks, the buildings. I feel I can almost hear them, all those impatient car horns, like flocks of birds in a poisoned jungle, I can see the pale, exasperated faces of the drivers trapped behind their wheels. They're all running, thinking they can't afford to waste a single second of their lives, when in fact they're already wasting most of them.

Elena reappears at the door. "Signor Romano, I forgot to tell you that your father has been trying to get hold of you again."

I take my eyes from the street, ready to ask her to make up an excuse, but when I turn to her I'm struck dumb. Instead of young Elena, a little old lady is standing in the doorway, back stooped, watching me in silence. She's dressed the same way, she's holding the same sheets of paper, but her skin is all wrinkled, and instead of the usual dark bob, there's a diaphanous halo of white hair. Her eyes have lost their light, they're buried in the thin, dark folds of her eyelids, and the way she's staring at me is disturbing.

"Please…" I implore her.

"What's the matter?" this old woman asks me in a cavernous voice, advancing slowly towards me, reaching out a pair of limp, shrivelled arms.

I'm shaking, I can't even cry for help. Her yellowed, hooklike fingers are coming closer, they're only a few centimetres from my hands.

"Leave me alone, please!" I scream, turning to face the window.

Now I can hear her heavy breathing behind me. She doesn't say anything, just breathes, then, suddenly, silence.

"Have I done something I shouldn't?"

It sounds like Elena's voice again. Maybe she's gone back to normal. I'm too scared to find out.

"I'm sorry," she says, "I didn't mean to scare you."

I'm terrified, I don't want to turn and find that she's a hundred years old. I don't want to go beyond that threshold and discover a decaying world, devoured by the destructive fury of time.

"Please answer me, Signor Romano. Aren't you feeling well?"

One, two, three, four, five. One, two, three, four, five. I need to convince myself that, when I turn, that repugnant old monster will have disappeared, and in her place I'll find Elena again.

One, two, three, four, five.

Elena, my young Elena, looks really worried. The last thing she expected was to see me bathed in tears and sweat. "What's happening to you?"

I feel my heart pumping at an unsustainable speed and my breath becoming ever heavier. "I'm scared," I confess, scrunching up my face in a childish grimace of complaint.

"Scared of what?"

"Of time," I say with tears in my eyes, unafraid now to seem ridiculous. "Time passing."

Then I collapse exhausted into the armchair.

Elena is really dismayed by now. "Would you like me to fetch you some water?"

"No. Call an ambulance, I need to see a doctor."

84

By the time the paramedics arrive, the office is in turmoil. The high-flying Signor Romano says he feels as if he's paralysed from head to foot and refuses to leave his chair.

It isn't easy to move me, because I'm completely stiff. The only thing I seem to be able to move is my mouth, I keep shouting at the paramedic, "Be careful! What's happening to me? Somebody explain what's happening to me!"

It's so embarrassing. I hear Elena stammering something about my being taken ill. "He was perfectly normal, then suddenly he became someone else. I can't explain it to you, he scared me."

Even the director has come running to help me, if his indignant air could be called helpful. Maybe he's only trying to imagine the consequences for our business of my being paralysed. "I have to go, keep me up to date with his condition," he says quickly before turning his back on me.

Barbara's here, too. She doesn't seem upset, only curious. She asks the paramedic for more information, then starts looking me up and down. Every time I give a spasm of pain, she just curls her lips and raises her eyebrows. "My God," she comments at a certain point, "if it was only stress it'd be worrying."

Elena has joined Paola, the switchboard operator, in the reception area and they've started chatting, I recognize their voices as I'm taken outside on a stretcher.

"You know you've lost weight," Elena is saying to her in a decidedly more relaxed tone.

"And you've done something to your face, you look better. Come on, tell me the truth, you know you can tell me... Oh my God, poor man. Let's hope he gets better soon."

In the ambulance, I gradually recover my strength: the pain wears off, leaving me with a slight feeling of pins and needles.

"It's passed," I tell the paramedic, making an attempt to stand up. I can't bear the thought of ending up in hospital.

"Calm down now… In a few minutes you'll be seeing a doctor."

"Maybe you didn't understand what I said, I feel much better, I don't want to see a doctor, I don't want to go to hospital. I'll contact my GP, you just have to take me home now."

I grab him by his coat, but he pulls my hand away and tries to keep me on the bed. It's one against two, and they're a lot stronger than I am.

"Just calm down," he says again, "there's no reason for you to get excited now."

"Listen, I'm telling you for the last time: let me out of here!"

"It's not as simple as that. Once we've got to the emergency department you can talk to whoever you need to, I'm not authorized to let you out of this vehicle."

With a final effort, I manage to grab him by the collar and scream, "Let me out, you son of a bitch!" My rage is uncontrollable, and this time the paramedic doesn't just hold me down on the bed, he gets his colleague to inject something into my veins, maybe a sedative.

"It's against the law…" I mutter, then I go completely limp and subside into a confused state.

I could never have imagined that this new accelerated perception of time might actually be a good thing. But the nightmare I'm living through seems to burn itself out quickly, and in no time at all I find myself lying on a bed in the emergency ward, while a bespectacled young doctor shines a light in my eyes and asks me to open my mouth wide.

"Can you speak?"

"I think so…" I reply, trying to move my sore tongue.

"What's your name?"

"Svevo. Svevo Romano."

"Good evening Svevo, I'm Dr Paoli. You were brought in because you weren't feeling at all well. Can you describe what happened?"

"What time is it?"

"Nine o'clock in the evening. Why are you so concerned with the subject of time? When you were semi-conscious, you kept saying over and over that you didn't have time. Are you afraid of being late for something?"

I don't trust this fellow. He's probably only just graduated.

"Just forget it."

"I'd really like you to tell me," he insists. "You'll feel better, you'll see."

I give him a hesitant glance, then decide to try to trust him. "I don't have any more time to live," I confess. "I have the sensation that everything is going too fast. It's time that's going too fast. Is that possible?"

The doctor raises his eyebrows, and a disorientated expression comes into his eyes. "We'll do a few tests, but in my opinion you had a panic attack. Brought on by stress, I'd say. What kind of work do you do?"

I shake my head, disappointed. "I'm an executive, but that's not the point."

"And how many hours a day do you work?"

I shrug. "I don't know, I have no idea."

He does the textbook thing and advises rest.

"I can go to my GP to have the tests done," I tell him as I get dressed. "Just tell me where I have to sign to get out of here."

"Are you in a hurry to get home?"

"Believe me, you would be, too, if you were in my position."

"And what *is* your position?"

"I told you, I'm someone who doesn't have any more time." I doubt I'll ever see him again. I don't want ever to come back here. It's a purgatory, with a smell of medicine impregnating your clothes and a line of white coats parading back and forth along antiseptic corridors. They look like angels, but they're cold, distant, always ready to announce some dreadful news.

Through my exhausted body, time is merely a rapid, meaning-less ticking. The end is knocking at the door, I haven't been able to handle it, it's brought me to my knees. Like a deadly cancer, You've taken possession of every cell of my existence. All I can do is surrender. And yet I feel an odd kind of strength growing inside me. The strength to say I've had enough, I need to get away from the office for a while. I have to take charge of what remains of my life.

9

O N THE FIRST DAY of my forced holiday, I thought I could do at least a few of the things I'd been putting off for more than a month. I wanted to go to the barber and then do a bit of shopping, but in the end I couldn't help putting everything off again. I need another coffee, it's my fourth today, I never even used to like it, but in the end I put that off, too, I'm just too exhausted and spend all day sprawled on the sofa, wearing only my pants.

Six hours fly by even more quickly when you just sit there in front of the television, not even managing to follow the plot of the film you're watching. The end credits arrive and I can't even remember the name of the main character. I have no idea when I'll get back to the office, the director asked Elena to persuade me to extend my leave indefinitely. I'm not bothered, the thing uppermost in my thoughts is the hallucinations. That old lady who looked like my secretary, my car in ruins: they were both so real.

I've made an appointment with De Santis, my GP. He's expecting me tomorrow morning, he told me over the phone that he'd like to do an EEG, possibly a scan. He wouldn't commit himself to a premature diagnosis, though he did say it might be a brain problem, perhaps a lesion. I assume my dissolute style of life has something to do with it, I shouldn't have overindulged in alcohol and drugs the way I have. I'm starting to see a lot of things in a new light. This apartment, for example, my beautiful penthouse of which I've always been so proud, courtesy of a top designer: I used to be crazy about all these weird things I spent a fortune on, but now these paintings and sculptures with their twisted shapes disturb me. They all seem like the decor for a nightmare.

At the end of the day, habit gets the better of me and I switch my mobile phone on again.

Predictably, it immediately starts ringing.

It's a withheld number. If I knew who was calling, I might not reply.

"Yes?"

"Svevo, it's Federico."

A brief silence follows. "Why are you withholding your number?"

"At least you replied. What's going on with you? You don't pick up your phone, you don't answer my messages. You've dropped out of sight. You don't even go to the gym any more. They told me you almost died in the Turkish bath. Should I be worried?"

"Goodbye, Federico."

"What are you doing? Aren't you going to say anything?"

"What do you want to know?"

"Well, for a start, how are you?"

It's incredible how many *how are yous* I've heard over the past month, all uttered in the same indifferent tone. But Federico's *how are you* is by far the most irritating.

"I've had a lot of work to do, we're about to finalize an important contract."

"Gaëlle has been trying to call you, too, she says you never answer, not even at work."

What do they still want from me? Are they hoping I'll give them my blessing? Or now that I'm out of the running, is everything too open and above board and therefore less exciting?

"Why, has she phoned you?"

Federico is good at evading the question. "She's coming to Italy next weekend. She called me to find out if I'd heard from you. We want to organize something, Claude Reinardt is DJ'ing at the Premium on Friday. How about dinner? Matteo and the others want to see you, too."

I feel like telling him to go to hell, but I hold back, I have to conserve my energy for more important battles. "I doubt I can make it, I'm otherwise engaged. A work commitment."

"Aren't you getting too stressed out with your work? What should I tell Gaëlle if she calls me? Maybe we can go and then you can join us later, if that's OK with you…"

If we were actors, this dialogue alone would deserve an Oscar nomination. "OK with me? Why shouldn't it be? Yes, I'll join you later if I can."

Someone has knocked at my door, what impeccable timing.

"I really have to go now."

"OK, bye. Hope to see you Friday."

What I hope is never to have anything to do with him again. I quickly slip on a dressing gown and go to open the door. I recognize her from her ponytail. She's put dark lipstick on and is wearing a pair of white patent-leather boots that make me think of a Japanese manga character, one of those porno nurses ready to take off their clothes at the drop of a hat. It's Donatella, my masseuse.

"Oh my God, am I disturbing you? Don't you remember? We were supposed to be having dinner together tonight."

91

With everything that's happened, I'd completely forgotten. "Of course," I say, trying to hide my embarrassment. "But… didn't we say nine o'clock?"

"I know, you're right, I'm a little bit late. But to say sorry I've brought a bottle of wine, it's the kind you really like."

I have nothing to eat in the apartment and it's already 9.30. I should never have invited her to dinner. It was my cock speaking.

"I'm afraid I'm a bit unprepared… You know, I haven't been well. I fell asleep a few hours ago and there's nothing ready. Shall we go to a restaurant?"

"No, what's the big deal, I'll make us a little something, you know I like cooking."

"Are you sure?"

Her smile tells me that for her, the question of food is of secondary importance tonight.

"You know what we'll do, then? I'll go and take a shower and leave you completely free in the kitchen, what do you think?"

"I don't think I can wait to have you taste a little delicacy of mine."

I'm still in the shower when Donatella comes and knocks at the door of the bathroom. "Everything OK, Svevo?"

"Yes, I'm sorry, I'll be right there."

"All I found in the cupboard was a tin of tomatoes," she tells me through the door. "I've made you some spaghetti."

"Good for you."

I haven't even managed to wash the shampoo out of my hair.

We finish eating, me as quickly as I can, and I barely have time to put my fork down on the plate when I find myself swept up by her enthusiasm. She's even more exciting naked than clothed.

Soft and scented, she's dying to have me inside her. It strikes me that a bit of healthy sex might help to distract me.

We collapse onto the sofa. She loosens her hair, laughing as happily as a child, but when she sits astride me she reminds me of one of those calendar pin-ups and I get very hard. I enter her with the haste of an animal, I move back and forth in a wild, primitive rhythm, desperate to come as quickly as possible, to empty myself of my anxieties, but I can't do it, because she gets tired almost immediately, she becomes passive and yielding, and makes me feel like a rapist. "No, no more," she begs me, wriggling out of my arms. "Are you on something tonight?"

Her reaction embarrasses me, though I'm still aroused. She's red in the face, she can hardly breathe. "You're incredible," she says, rearranging her hair, "but I can't take it any more… I have to get up early tomorrow morning, I really should go."

According to the clock behind her, nearly two hours have gone by since we finished eating. God Almighty, in real time two hours have already passed, which hasn't done me any favours. "I'm not feeling well," I say. "Yes, I think it's best if you go."

"Oh, my God. You aren't well. I'm sorry, where are my manners?"

"It isn't your fault, really."

"Look, if you like, I'll stay a while longer, we could even carry on, I don't mind…"

I gently put a hand on her lips to silence her. I'm still aroused by her perfume and I'm sorry to have to deprive myself of her wonderful body so soon, but I don't have any intention of torturing anybody. I stroke her face and reassure her that she's behaved perfectly. "I'm really not feeling well, Donatella. But we can meet another time, if you want. It was a very pleasant evening, the spaghetti was delicious."

SIMONA SPARACO

Donatella returns my smile. I help her to get dressed, walk her to the door, and say goodbye.

It isn't easy to describe what I'm living through, to go into details with sufficient clarity. De Santis, my doctor, has a lot of questions, he even asks me to tell him everything a second time. The story I've just told is grotesque, and the fact that I'm in his clinic certainly doesn't make things any easier. I hate doctors' clinics, I don't find anything reassuring about them. All those drawings of the human body, those indecipherable charts, as if there was a logical explanation for everything, while I feel like a blind man groping in a room he doesn't know.

I also tell him about You, about the fact that in my life I've never believed in anything that wasn't tangible or couldn't at least be experienced physically, and yet I'm convinced that Father Time exists somewhere, maybe in a parallel universe, and is constantly controlling its flow.

"Father Time, you said?"

He looks puzzled, but is more serious than I thought he would be.

I nod. "That's right, Father Time."

De Santis sighs. "You're going to have a brain scan," he says, with a somewhat paternal air. "It'll tell us if there are any traumas or lesions that may have provoked an alteration in your sensory perceptions."

He's known me since I was a child, he looked after my mother before my family moved to Turin, I know he's worried, even though he's trying hard not to show it.

"Svevo, tell me the truth. Do you take drugs? Hallucinogens, LSD, cocaine, or even just a bit of grass every now and again?"

94

"Joints make me overexcited, Francesco. I only do coke. A couple of times I've dropped a bit of acid, and this summer I had some hallucinogenic mushrooms."

In other circumstances I wouldn't have been so honest, but my health is at stake and I don't care what he thinks of me.

"How often do you use cocaine?"

His professionalism, rather than any affection he may have for me, obliges him not to make any comments and to keep calm and reserved.

"Until a month ago, maybe two or three times a week," I admit. "But I've stopped now, and just the thought of trying again wipes me out." That's no addict's promise, I certainly don't need to go any faster than I already am.

De Santis remains silent, I think he's trying to restrain himself. In a context like this, any kind of reprimand would be completely inappropriate.

He asks me to follow him, the scanning room should be ready. He makes me sit on a long contraption that looks like a coffin, they immobilize me with a device that fits over my forehead and tell me to keep calm. There's a microphone, so that I can communicate with them if I need to.

When the machine starts, I quickly slide inside the tube. The whole thing lasts about ten minutes, of my time of course, during which my ears are battered by sound vibrations in a stop and start rhythm. It consoles me to know that outside this room a group of doctors is closely examining every corner of my brain.

When it's over, I get dressed again and De Santis walks me back to his office.

Now I'm waiting silently on my chair while my friend the doctor is at his desk, going through my results.

At last he breaks the silence. "Svevo," he says, his tone one of relief, "you don't have what I was fearing. If you want my expert opinion, I'd say it was a freak incident, caused by stress, and perhaps also drug abuse. But you've been lucky, you haven't suffered any visible damage. For now I can only advise you to make an appointment with a colleague of mine, his name is Giuliani and he's an excellent analyst. I'm sure he can be of help to you."

"I only want this thing to end as soon as possible."

"It'll end as soon as you realize that it's your head that's creating all this. It might be a kind of autosuggestion, and the only way to fight it is with will-power."

"It's no suggestion, Francesco, believe me. It's real, at least as real as anything in my life until now."

"You're physically healthy, so the only thing I can prescribe is tranquillizers. But listen to me, make an appointment with Giuliani. There's no shame in it. As I said, he may be able to help you."

When I'm at the door, De Santis lets out a sigh, as if up to now he's been holding back, and asks me about my father. "Have you heard from him lately?" His expression is grave. He knows my father and I have never been on especially good terms, that I don't see him often and don't have much respect for him, and I'm sure he disapproves. Like my relatives, he may have hoped we'd become reconciled over the years.

"Yes, I spoke to him on the phone... Don't look at me like that."

De Santis won't let go. "At a time like this, his presence may be of help to you, have you thought of that? I'm sure he needs you, too. I'm saying this as a friend: now that you know how pitiless time can be, don't leave things unresolved."

I smile at him: let him believe I'll follow his advice if he wants to. But my soul is divided into many compartments, and my father has ended up in the darkest and most cramped. The walls are long and narrow, and I've tried to take him out of there many times, but never succeeded.

When I get back to my car and make ready to plunge back into the unstoppable flow of the city, I find myself thinking that it's done me good to talk to De Santis after all, even though I would have preferred a concrete answer, however tragic. An enemy I could fight, not just a suspicion of madness. I refuse to believe that my mind is doing everything by itself, that the hallucinations and the strange things that are happening to time are just inventions of my sick psyche. How can I get used to a perception of reality in which things and people suddenly get older, or to a strong relentless wind called time that sweeps everything away without distinction?

So here I am, stuck in an uncomfortable leather armchair, facing an elderly, white-haired psychiatrist with a vague air, who can't even find his pen. He's supposed to be someone who can deal with even the most difficult situations but he's going crazy looking for a missing pen. Not what you might call an encouraging start. But I have to trust him, you've got to start somewhere.

"When and how did the first disturbances manifest themselves?"

Here goes. "I was on a plane to Paris. I should tell you that… well, let's just say I'm afraid of flying."

He listens to me, nodding from time to time but never interrupting. All at once, he starts looking at his watch, I realize that his face has changed expression, he's assumed a manner that's definitely not very professional, I'd even say he seems disorientated, as if he was wandering in completely unexplored terrain and hasn't

97

the least idea what to do. If he hadn't been recommended to me by De Santis, I'd advise him to just concentrate on looking for his pen.

By the time the session is over, I already know I'll never see him again. It's all too obvious that I'm in a hurry to say goodbye and go, but who cares?

Two days later it's the turn of Federico's former shrink: I found the number in my diary and phoned him to fix an appointment.

"Time. Ah, time…"

That's how he begins, after listening to me for a few moments.

"Time, like space, is an element intrinsic to our universe and therefore only exists in relation to matter, in its manifestation as mass and energy. Outside matter, it could even be said that time doesn't exist…"

He launches into an elaborate speech on the subject which, predictably, I find myself unable to follow. He moves casually from the sea of time in esoteric physics to the possibility of time travel. I fail to see what any of this has to do with my problem.

I really can't stand it a minute longer, so as soon as he gives me a prescription for a series of homoeopathic remedies, I quickly say goodbye. If nothing else, I now have a clearer psychological picture of the man who used to be my best friend.

10

GAËLLE IS IN ROME this evening. She and Federico are having dinner somewhere in the centre of town. I imagine them together, on that brightly coloured merry-go-round their lives resemble, and I gradually realize what a profound state of solitude I've been living in. Not the forced solitude of these last few months, not the isolation, the abyss that has just swallowed me up, but that carousel of laughter, pleasantries, music, mood shifts and addictions. Empty, meaningless words, eyes that hide unknown abysses. I see everything with disarming clarity now. We're like floating bubbles, incapable of communicating. We're so afraid of bursting that we refuse all true contact with each other.

Despite everything, out of pure survival instinct, I have to regain some kind of control over my life. I want to go out, see people. Staying shut up at home doesn't help me slow things down, and besides, any party, even the most pointless, will pass quickly anyway. So I decide to summon up courage and call Luca, an old friend who doesn't move in the same circles any more. I ask him if he has any plans for the evening and he suggests an informal dinner at a restaurant on the outskirts of Rome, the kind of restaurant where the fettuccine tastes of fresh eggs and the only wine served is house wine.

"Isn't Federico coming?" he asks me.

"I haven't seen him for a while."

"Did something happen?"

"Nothing serious," I say quickly. "That life was starting to tire me."

Luca uses this remark as an excuse to launch into a lecture. "I always said you were overdoing it. I don't know how you managed to keep up the pace. I guess it was fun, but in small doses. In the end I was waking up in the morning feeling as limp as a rag. Not to mention the problems I was having at work. I was heavily in debt."

I have no wish to go further into the matter, let alone to contradict him. "You're right," is all I say. "Listen, what time did you say this evening?"

"About nine. The restaurant is called Il Cacciatore. Are you coming in your car or would you like me to pick you up?"

"I feel like driving. I'll see you there."

There are places in the country, sometimes even quite close to a large metropolis, that smell healthy and clean and make you want to pull the window down, fill your lungs and let the wind caress your face. If only the country air could help me get back to normal.

I had to leave home quite early. My watch says 8.45, the road is clear, and there aren't too many bends. I'm going very fast, I don't want to get there half an hour late.

Il Cacciatore. My headlamps light up the sign, which is an old plywood board with a bearded man in a hunting cap drawn on it, hanging from two small chains that squeak as they move in the wind. It's the kind of sign you used to see. I park my Aston Martin on the gravel in front of the steps leading up to the restaurant, jump out and quickly run to the entrance.

The place seems nice and even quite crowded. If Federico was here, at this point we'd exchange a knowing glance: a couple of overweight, badly dressed families, a table of young boys covered in tattoos, and a few whores in miniskirts.

The group who are expecting me for dinner are sitting at a table next to a stone fireplace hung round with sausages: Luca and his new friends, who all look intellectual and well-behaved.

"Ah, here's Svevo! Do you know each other? Paolo, Marco, Ginevra and Susanna."

"Hello, everyone."

I sit down next to Luca. "Is anybody else coming?"

"We're just waiting for Giorgio and Isabelle," he replies. "They'll be here soon."

Isabelle. For some reason, the name brings me up short. "Who's Isabelle?"

"A friend. Don't give me that look, Svevo, I can tell you right now she's not your type, even though she's French. She must be about your age and has a one-year-old daughter. Plus, Giorgio's fallen madly in love with her."

A moment later, the door of the restaurant opens. I don't know how to explain it, but suddenly everything disappears except for those eyes and that haze of red hair. She advances slowly, almost swaying, step after step, until she reaches our table and gracefully slips off her shawl.

"Svevo, do you know Isabelle?"

No, I don't know her, but I would've liked to get to know her the first time I saw her, at the airport, before I got on the flight that would change my life.

She smiles at me. Luminous, transparent eyes, like freshly washed windows, small segments of sky. She says hello to the rest of the table, and with each gesture she makes, each word she

101

utters, I can't help looking at her. There's something magnetic about the way she moves and speaks.

I'm in luck, because she sits down just opposite me.

She isn't a classic beauty, at least not what passes for a classic beauty these days. She looks as if she's stepped straight out of one of those eighteenth-century French prints: a full, not entirely regular mouth covered with freckles, like the rest of her face, a high, commanding forehead. "Haven't we met before?" she asks me.

I decide to lie. "I thought so, too, but I can't remember where."

"Svevo, right?"

"Yes, Isabelle."

The laughter and chatter at the table gradually increase in volume, while this unknown woman and I continue looking at each other in silence. Every now and again she turns to listen to what somebody is saying, answer a question or smile at the idiot who's sitting next to her, this Giorgio she came in with, who can't stop flattering her, pouring wine and water for her, serving her starters, lighting and relighting the candle when it goes out. He seems so proud of his task as knight errant, but from what I can tell he appears to know he has no hope.

As for me, I haven't lavished any ridiculous compliments on her, I'm not trying in any way to seduce her. I'm only searching for something interesting to say, and for the first time I'm not in a hurry, I'm not obsessed with the problem of time. I've decided to ignore the clock, I want the evening to follow its natural course. However absurd it is, I have the strange, inexplicable feeling that I'm on the verge of something, that something new is about to start. I've become a child again and I haven't yet committed any sins. She doesn't scare me, she's like a regenerating force. She could be the one, among so many, who's ready to join me without any fear of bursting. I imagine the two us, floating, one large bubble.

"I have an image in my head of you with a child in your arms, a little girl."

"I'm a mother. My daughter's thirteen months."

"So it's true. We have met before."

"Apparently, yes."

Luca gives me a sideways glance.

"Are the two of you married?" I ask, indicating Giorgio.

"The two of us? No, we're just friends. I'm not married."

Giorgio can't hide his disappointment. That "we're just friends" must have made him choke on his bruschetta.

"Maybe we met at work," I insist, hoping to find out something about her life.

"I'm a photographer, when I'm not a mother, which means not often."

"A photographer? That's interesting."

"I used to do travel stuff," she says, slipping a breadstick out of the packet, "now I'm in the fashion field."

"I like photographs. These days, with mobile phones and everything, anybody can take them, our whole lives are filled with them."

"It's a pity everything's digital now," she replies, biting into her breadstick. "I like to touch photographs, to smell them."

At this point, Giorgio butts into the conversation. "I agree with you," he says. But Isabelle doesn't take her eyes off me.

For the first time in I don't know how long, I find myself involved in an interesting conversation. We talk about the fact that technology is apparently more democratic: today everyone can aspire to perfection, at least in a photograph. In fashion, she says, retouching is almost obligatory, but she also tells me that when she worked in Paris, for a scientific monthly, it was the most authentic photos that gave her the greatest satisfaction. "In journalism, you almost always look for the truth," she says. I can see the panoramas she describes to me, the populations of those remote villages where she spent much of her youth, taking photographs.

She must be more than thirty but, I think, not yet forty. She certainly doesn't have the youthful freshness I usually go crazy over in a woman. And yet I have the impression she knows better than anyone how to wear the time that passes. She doesn't seem bothered by the small lines around her eyes, and she clearly hasn't resorted to anything unnatural to try to stretch them. She doesn't smoke, she doesn't wear jewellery, her style is minimal, clean and elegant, somewhat old-fashioned. She doesn't have a touch of make-up on, except maybe a bit of lipgloss, which reflects the quivering light of the candles as she moves her lips. I notice her slender fingers, her short, unpolished nails. I like looking at them as she gesticulates or arranges her hair behind her ears. There can be great sensuality even in an ordinary gesture like that.

I don't ask her anything about her past, like how she came to be alone in Italy with such a small child, but I do ask her to talk to me about her daughter, whose name is Giulia, she just told me.

"Giulia is…" her eyes light up and she looks in the air, searching for the right words. "Giulia is a force of nature," she says at last. "She calls me mam*ma*, with the accent on the second syllable just like in French, and she's always smiling."

"Isabelle, do you want to taste a little of my pasta?" Giorgio interrupts us again, this time with a touch of impatience.

"No, thanks," she replies. "Mine will be here soon."

Soon, she said. I haven't been served either. And we're only on the starters. I thought much more time had passed. I feel extraordinarily relaxed, I can't believe this is really happening. I almost have the impression that my time is finally slowing down.

You're going more slowly. I like to imagine You've stopped to look at us.

I lift my wrist to my ear and start listening to my watch ticking calmly. For the first time, it gives me an incredible sense of peace.

"Is your watch broken?" Isabelle asks curiously.

"I think so," I reply, almost euphorically. "I really think so."

I suggest a toast. Just like that, without any reason, just the two of us, an excuse to smile at her in silence. Actually, what I'd like to do is thank her, I have the feeling this sudden sense of relaxation that's come over me is all down to her. Isabelle raises her glass, the others look at us in surprise. This cheap red is the best wine I've ever tasted and this toast is the most important one of my life. Nobody knows I'm toasting my own recovery, my hope that I've got back to normal.

A veil of lightness comes to rest on all things, on the fat, badly dressed women, the tattooed boys, the suggestive looks of the whores, even the strings of sausages over the fireplace. In the meantime I continue talking to her, this woman who knows how to slow down time.

"So," I say, "Giulia's always smiling."

"Always. Every day she learns something new. My God, it seems to me only yesterday I was expecting her, she makes me feel..."

She doesn't finish the sentence, but I understand perfectly well what she means. She can't imagine how I live with that feeling every day, and in the most exaggerated, nerve-wracking manner possible.

"Time flies," she concludes with a shrug. She's so serene about it, it's almost infuriating.

"And doesn't that scare you a bit?"

"No, no more than a lot of other things. I know I've used my time as best I could, and now that I have my daughter I don't want to miss even a moment of her life. Sometimes I imagine her as she'll be when she's a woman, and I feel so proud of her, I can hardly wait for that day to arrive."

I listen to her and I'd like her to take me by the hand, as you do with children when they get restless.

In the meantime, Giorgio must have reached the end of his tether. He tries to butt in again. "I'd like to propose a toast, too," he says. "To children."

Everybody raises their glasses. I'm probably looking a bit puzzled, Isabelle must have noticed. She joins in the toast, without any enthusiasm, then asks me, "What about you? Are you married?"

I smile. The idea has never even occurred to me, which is no secret to anyone. "No, I'm not married."

"So no children, I assume."

"No children."

There's nothing judgemental about her attitude, the way she looks at me is reassuring, at least as reassuring as the discovery that I finished my pasta before the others.

"Do you work hard?"

"Quite hard."

My life is what she's interested in now. I've never thought about it before, but I'd like to dig into it and find something that makes it more interesting. I have the feeling that my work, my clubbing, my vices are as far away from her world as it's possible to be. All at once, the table seems to grow between the two of us. I know I might scare her off. I'm not like this Giorgio who keeps pouring her wine, I'm not a good person. Some people seem to be enveloped in a halo of benevolence, a halo that prevents anger from turning nasty and becoming hate. In my life, though, anger has become indifference. I'm capable of committing despicable acts and dismissing them as if they were nothing to do with me. I learnt betrayal at school. At the age of twelve, I persuaded Alice, with whom I shared a desk, to take off her knickers in front of my friends. Every time she tried to push our hands away from her thighs we would laugh, with that taste for wickedness which at the age of twelve may appear innocent. One day I told her I loved her, all I wanted in return was to know what people meant when they talked about sex. A week later, I shifted my attentions to her best friend, whose skin smelt of fruit.

I imagine that if Isabelle looked in my memory and found Alice's eyes, just as I remember them, she'd stop smiling at me. The point is that her smile is like a hand that comes to rest on your back, like a push. Perhaps for the first time since I came into the world, I'm staring into the abyss of my own conscience.

By now the candles are flickering and the evening is winding to its end. Everyone is walking towards their own cars. Kisses, words of farewell. I don't lose sight of her for a moment. I'm waiting for her to approach me and say something.

"Goodbye, Svevo. It's been nice meeting you."

I take her hand and she squeezes mine in return. All I can find to say is a whispered "See you soon". I'm usually more talkative, more self-confident. If it was any other woman, I'd already have her phone number in my pocket.

She hesitates, as if she wants to ask me something, but Giorgio is still calling her. I see her get in his car and I can't do anything about it. I've become afraid of time again, I sense You're about to resume Your race and I don't know how to stop You.

When I get back behind the wheel, my mind clouds over and all I can do is press my foot down on the accelerator. All the same,

I have the feeling I'll see her again. There must be a reason she's entered my life at this particular juncture, a reason she's managed to slow down my time.

By the time I get to the garage, my watch has taken a leap forward and it's already two o'clock in the morning. The whole evening reminds me of one of those music videos where some of the images are speeded up and others are suddenly slowed down, and when they slow down she comes towards me, swaying, with her haze of red hair.

Just before I put my key in the lock, I hear a woman crying behind me.

11

W HEN I TURN, I see Gaëlle, curled up on the mat by the door that leads up to the terrace of the building. It's the first time I've ever seen her crying.

"Gaëlle, what are you doing here?" I ask, sitting down next to her. "What's the matter?"

She looks so defenceless, my first instinct is to put my arms around her. But Gaëlle aims at me those sapphires she has instead of eyes and asks me to switch off the light on the stairs. "I don't want to give you the satisfaction of seeing me in this state." Her tone is sharp and irritable. She doesn't give me time to open my mouth. "Look, I know you're enjoying this."

I shake my head, I'd like to tell her she's wrong.

"Don't be a hypocrite."

"It's the last thing on my mind," I reassure her in a paternal tone that doesn't even sound like me.

"You like it, don't you?" she insists. "Seeing me crumble like this. You can't fool me, I know how your mind works. You vanished because this is what you wanted, to see me crumble at last." She throws me a fiery gaze, then immediately turns away.

She's pale, there are rings under her eyes, and her lipstick is smudged.

"What are you talking about?"

She gives a nervous little laugh. "I hate you," she says. "And to think I lost my head over you." More impatient than ever, she gets up and comes and stands in front of me. "Why don't you say anything?"

She doesn't give me time.

"You're really hurting me," she says, with a look in her eyes that in any other circumstances I'd find disarming. "I did everything I could to stay with you, even deluded myself I could be satisfied with that kind of non-relationship. But now I can't stand it any more..."

"Who are you?" I'd like to ask, but once again I don't have time, because suddenly Gaëlle opens the door of my apartment. "I'm sleeping with you," she announces, walking in. "I want to fuck you all night long."

If everything was normal, a scene like this would have excited me more than you could imagine. Not this time.

"I know you like it when I talk like that," she continues, but it's as if she's addressing someone who doesn't exist any more.

She touches my neck, first with her fingertips, then with her lips, which are cold and damp. I remain rigid, distant. She bursts into tears again. Because of my accelerated time, her behaviour comes across as psychotic, which of course it may actually be. "I shouldn't have..." she stammers. "I knew I was wrong, but I wanted to hurt you in some way... I didn't think anything would make me feel better."

She's on the verge of a confession, which is the last thing I'd have expected of her. I make an effort to appear surprised. "What are you talking about?"

She wipes her tears. "I'm talking about Federico," she says. "I slept with him."

I know this is the image of her that will remain with me, perhaps the most genuine: her head held high, that angry, accusing look in her eyes, even as she admits to a nasty gesture like that.

"Did you hear what I said?" Her voice rises in pitch. "I slept with your best friend!"

I give her a slap, just to make her stop. Shouting it at the top of her voice won't make it seem like my fault.

I wonder if two months ago I would have forgiven her, or if I would have continued sleeping with her, even knowing. Now I'd only like to pick her up out of the hole she's rushed headlong into. She seems like a little insect that's dying, her wings crumpled, too weak to fly again.

She lays her cheek on my chest and at last closes her eyes. I hold her in my arms, while she asks me to understand her. "I did it to take everything from you," she says, "the way you took everything from me."

She's fragile, a beautiful orchid deprived of water. Her hair is unkempt, and she's breathing heavily. "Don't leave me."

I don't know who she is. All those nights of sex, those forbidden games, the shameless phone calls and messages, and now I don't have the slightest idea who she is. It's incredible, the distance I've ended up putting between myself and people.

She presses her lips to mine with a new urgency that's unusual in her.

A moment ago she told me she knew how my mind worked. Who was that man you filled your head with strategies for, Gaëlle? Tell me, I'd like to know too. How did I look at you, what did I say to you? This kiss is pointless. You know that too, don't you?

I move her away from me and ask her to go, to go now.

She sweeps her hair back from her face and again pours out all her resentment on me. I lose the thread of her attacks. "You're not like me," she says. She mentions my inability to love, my superficiality, the drugs, the boredom, the pain. "If you've got to your age like that, I doubt you'll ever be able to change. You're just a poor bastard."

Then she opens the door and leaves my apartment without another glance.

In a moment, faster than ever, Gaëlle is out of my life. I wonder if she was ever part of it. Of everything she's said, that unstoppable flow of words she's poured over me, one truth remains: I was never able to love her. I've never been capable of loving anybody. The most alarming thing is that now everything seems devoid of meaning. It hardly matters that sex is something that's over in an instant, that a beautiful girl turns suddenly into an old woman, or that my baby is nothing but a dusty relic. In this exhausting race, my life is overtaking me, and almost everything that was part of it leaves me completely indifferent.

The morning light is coming in through the living-room window. Another night has flown past.

I'm exhausted. I've almost lost the will to start running again.

But Isabelle and what I felt when I saw her last night oblige me not to give up.

I have to find her. Somehow, I have to start living again.

It's the middle of the day, and I'm out and about in the city trying to attend to all the things I've left unresolved. Federico keeps calling me on my mobile, he's filled my voicemail with messages, but I have no intention of calling him back.

Instead, I call Luca. "I had a great time with all of you the other night," I tell him, trying to get straight to the point before the time at my disposal is used up. "I hope there'll be an opportunity to—"

"What are you talking about, Svevo? Of course there will be. I had a great time, too."

"There's something I wanted to ask you," I go on, my tone changing. "Tell me about Isabelle... Do you know how I can find her?"

Luca's tone changes, too: he's on the defensive. "Svevo, listen, I don't want to get into that. Giorgio's a friend."

"But they're not together."

"No, but he likes her a lot. And I think he's right for her, we just have to give her time."

"You're talking like a priest, Luca. Let me put it another way. You know me, you know I tire quickly of things, but this time it's different. I have to see her again, it's important."

Luca sticks to his guns, and for a specific reason. "I also know your hang-ups," he says. "Isabelle's a nice girl. Believe me, she's not for you."

"For once, you have to trust me," I insist. "You know I don't bullshit, you have to admit that at least."

He sighs. He's still reluctant, not to mention all the time I'm making him waste.

I suggest a compromise. "Let's do something, you give me a clue, I don't know, somewhere she does her shopping, the place where she works. Give me just one thing, I'll see to the rest."

Luca hesitates some more, but finally gives in. "She takes her daughter for a walk in Villa Balestra park most afternoons."

"Thanks, Luca. You're a friend."

At lunchtime, I'm sitting on a bench with a roll in my hand—my usual meal over the past three months—waiting for her.

It's quite a small park, finding her shouldn't be too difficult.

113

It's quite windy today, though, so she might have decided not to come. The thought of coming here every day doesn't bother me, waiting has become easier since the minutes have started flying by so quickly. I have a weight on my stomach like a stone, but I don't really care. I haven't felt like this since I was young: maybe the first time I had sex or when I graduated.

A smell of grass smoke reaches me on the wind. A group of young guys close to the little fountain are smoking joints and listening to the Beatles. This park doesn't seem like the best place to take a little girl for a walk. I assume Isabelle lives in the neighbourhood. Instinctively I glance at the buildings beyond the railings, trying to imagine her apartment, the style she chose to decorate it in. I walk to the far end of the park, behind the cafeteria, where some ladies are sipping tea. There's a little playground, a skating lane shaded by pines and a few benches with words scratched on them, some little boys are hopping on the gravel, a dog runs beside them, but there's no sign of Isabelle and Giulia.

Soon the sun starts going down. It's the first sunset I've happened to see in this new dimension. In an instant, the sun is swallowed up by the horizon, as if You're in a hurry to hide it from me and are forcing it down with a big, invisible hand. The sky is tinged with red as quickly as a tablecloth is stained with wine when you knock over a bottle by accident. All this can't just be the result of my imagination. My mind alone wouldn't be able to devise something like this.

I leave the park and the pitiless spectacle You've just offered me. How long will it last? I look up at the sky, now calm and full of stars, and shout, "What are You waiting for?"

"Maybe it's too late," I mutter to myself, before getting back in my car.

12

I 'VE BEEN BACK to Villa Balestra every day for two weeks. The same disquieting spectacle every time, but no sign of Isabelle. Luca doesn't answer my phone calls any more. Almost nobody is looking for me. I'm learning to live with my lateness, with the constant race that my life has become.

The day I go back to work, I find myself impatiently pressing the button of the lift, after dismissing Paola, the switchboard operator, with a hurried greeting, when all she wanted was to know about my convalescence. I'm getting back on the right track. This time I can't stop any more, whatever happens, whatever hallucination waylays me.

"So you're back…" Smiling, Barbara sticks her head round the door of my office. "Had a good time, did you?"

I make an effort to tease her the way I used to. "Consider it maternity leave." I've equalized, one-all.

She laughs, then comes in and gives me a hug. "Joking apart, you gave us a real fright."

A fright they quickly recovered from, apparently, seeing that none of them even bothered to phone me.

"Do you really think you can manage?" she insists, ironically.

"You're radiant… Why? Is there any news?"

She gives me a broad smile. "Apparently there's a promotion in the air."

I must have opened my eyes wide.

"At least that's how I chose to interpret the director's words," Barbara continues, "when he summoned me to his office and showered me with praise over the way I handled a couple of things."

"Congratulations," I say, trying to maintain my usual tone. "At this rate you'll be taking my place."

Barbara, too, chooses to continue on the path of irony. "Anyway, you've always known what my intentions were," she says. "Get rid of a man like you and replace him with a woman like me. You know what a blow that is for all male chauvinists?"

"Sounds encouraging. But don't crow too soon."

"And don't get to your appointments too late."

I find her sense of humour totally inappropriate at a moment like this, and can't help thinking of the look of indifference on her face the day I was taken ill. I'd always thought she wasn't quite as cynical as she wanted me to believe, that our constant teasing was just an innocent game. But I was wrong, completely wrong. I'm certain she'd climb over anybody or anything to get that promotion.

"I won't bother you any more," she says. "How about grabbing a coffee later?"

I nod and give a little smile, while in my mind I see hundreds of cups of coffee flying across a counter, and hands trying to grab them. I smile again, then say goodbye.

I have to fly, too, I have to hurry. One hand on the computer, the other on my mobile. If I had another hand, I'd even be able to hold the receiver of the telephone without having to wedge it between my neck and my shoulder. I have to be quick. I write a message, move an appointment, tell Elena to send a fax. Right now, she could fall down in a faint and I wouldn't even notice, so determined am I to finish as soon as possible. I want to be back in that park before it gets dark.

I have to wait for a week, another very quick week, before I see Isabelle again. At ten o'clock on Monday morning I go to my bank for a quick chat with the manager. For once I arrive ahead of time, but out of breath. At work, I'm slowly and laboriously regaining ground, and I've arranged another meeting with Righini at lunchtime, the director will be there, too. The situation is more complicated than it was a month ago, Righini has had other offers . and has retreated from his previous position, but we're still in negotiation and the game is far from over. In the afternoon I have another important meeting with a young local councillor about that old question of the building permits, which is still unresolved. It's going to be a difficult day, not that there have been any easy ones lately. My impatience is tangible, I don't want to risk being distracted for a moment and finding that it's already the middle of the afternoon. I can't afford that today.

Anyway, it's a good thing I got here a bit early and that the manager is keeping me waiting, because when I look around I see her.

I always knew it would happen sooner or later, but it's like a sudden shock: Isabelle sitting at a table, busy signing some papers. She's wearing a light raincoat and her curly hair is gathered in a bun. Her daughter is waiting for her silently in the pushchair.

"Giulia?"

I approach the little girl, smiling, and she returns my smile with a disarming and quite unexpected sweetness.

117

Isabelle, too, seems happy to see me. "It's you! How are you?"

Fine, now that I've found you again in such an unpredictable way. Now that I can stop and look at you and catch my breath.

"What are you doing around here?"

"This has always been my bank," she says.

I'm surprised to discover that we've shared the same branch without knowing it. God knows how many times we've both been in the queue, one behind the other, like that day at the airport, without our eyes ever meeting. When it comes down to it, life is a long series of queues, waiting for an encounter.

"I've been thinking about her future," she continues, glancing at her daughter. "A savings account."

"A good idea," I say, imagining the day Giulia will come here to take advantage of her mother's foresight, as if it's going to happen tomorrow. Isabelle puts the forms in her handbag, grabs her shopping bags, grabs the handle of the pushchair and is about to say goodbye. But I have no intention of letting her escape again. I offer to help her, like that first time at the airport, and she accepts.

"But I thought you were waiting to see someone."

"It isn't urgent," I reply, leaving the bank with her bags in my hand.

The only thing in my life right now is you, Isabelle. I want to see if you can slow everything down again.

I walk with her through the neighbourhood. Turning a corner, we find an ice-cream parlour and a small lawn. We sit down in the open air.

It wasn't a chance occurrence, limited to that evening. When I'm with her, time quite simply stops racing. The ice cream doesn't melt, my watch says 10.05, and the clouds in the sky remain where they are.

I feel that for her, too, it's more than simple attraction, she's looking for something in me. We're scrutinizing each other as we talk, moving around each other in a series of seductive little skirmishes that make me feel good, make me feel better than I've felt in a long time. Gradually, I forget about time, I'm sure she'll remind me of it sooner or later, when she has to go home to feed her daughter, and then I'll go to my appointments. The only thing I'm certain of is that it's still morning and that there's suddenly no need to hurry any more.

Isabelle is a caring mother. You can tell that from the way she wipes the chocolate from her daughter's mouth. I learn a lot about her from these maternal gestures, like that day at the airport, when she made me feel I wanted to be in Giulia's place. She makes people want to be children again.

I ask her to tell me something about her life. She says she came to Italy for love and stayed out of respect. "Respect for Giulia, who was born here, and who has the right to live the life I dreamt for her when I brought her into the world."

Giulia's father is an architect. Apparently their relationship unravelled between all those endless meetings and business trips of his. At a certain point they realized they couldn't keep going on the way they had been. It was painful but inevitable, she admits. "Luca told me you also work hard and have an active social life." There's no trace of reprimand in her voice, although I have the feeling Luca wasn't all that complimentary about me.

She wants me to tell her a typical day of mine. I don't hold back. I describe in broad outlines what my work consists of, what I do in my spare time, as if I still had any, and the life I led until not so long ago, when almost every evening I'd book a table in some fashionable restaurant or club, obviously sparing her the more regrettable details.

"So apparently, you spend almost all your time sitting at a table," she remarks, with an amused smile. "Behind your desk by day, at tables in restaurants and clubs at night. Even your weightlifting is mainly done sitting down. Maybe that's why you stopped?"

I've never thought about it like that. I try to regain a few points by taking her observation as a joke. I'm encouraged by the fact that she's still looking at me the same way. On paper, I may seem a bit off-putting, I know, I'm the type of man a woman like her ought to run a mile from, but I have the impression that Isabelle doesn't look at things the way other people do, that she sees beyond appearances.

Suddenly Giulia starts crying. She's been walking on her own and has fallen on the ground. She hasn't hurt herself, but you know how children are, she gets upset easily. "Giulia, come here, darling. Let mummy give you a kiss... It's all right." But Giulia continues crying. "She's tired," Isabelle says. "I have to take her home. It's best if we go."

I don't want to know what time it is and give up this miraculous state of serenity. I still have time for the lunch with Righini, I know. Maybe that's the secret, I have to keep thinking that there's no hurry, I mustn't let my anxieties overwhelm me. Time goes more quickly when I think I don't have enough of it.

"Are you free tomorrow?" Isabelle asks me as I walk her to her car.

"I'll be free after lunch."

"What a pity. Tomorrow morning I'm going shopping at the market near where I live, and it's something I very much like doing in company."

"That's an excellent idea," I say, implying that I'll be there, and that for her sake I'd get out of any prior commitment.

I help her to arrange the pushchair and the shopping bags in the boot. "Do you ever go to Villa Balestra?" I ask her instinctively, just before saying goodbye. "I mean… do you ever take Giulia for a stroll there?"

"Villa Balestra?" she replies in surprise. "No. Why should I? I live in the centre."

So Luca just made me waste more time, the last thing I needed in this situation.

No sooner does Isabelle drive away than my mobile phone starts ringing, in that rapid, insistent way that makes me think of a firing squad, and an anxious shudder shakes my chest. I can't afford another leap forward in time.

"Romano, it's Righini."

His tone is the reasonably impatient one I've learnt to recognize, and can mean only one thing: I'm late for our appointment again.

Resigned, I wait for his outburst of temper, instead of which he surprises me by saying, "I'll be ten minutes late. I wanted to tell you well in advance, though I'm usually the one who has to wait for you."

"Why, what time is it?"

"11.30. There's time, Romano, there's time."

13

I N THE CAR, on the way to the restaurant, all I could do was think again about Isabelle and the incredible feelings she arouses in me. But it was no good, because You started racing again, faster than ever.

Once again I arrived late, I practically didn't touch any of the food or follow a word of what Righini and the director were saying. All the way through lunch, they kept glancing at me uneasily. My nervous state, my inability to handle the situation, was all too obvious.

Before going back to the office, the director, who's managed, without my help, to arrange a meeting to sign the contract next week, is forthright in his criticism of my undignified behaviour. "We can talk about it more calmly once we're back in the office." I try to make him understand that I don't have time for his lectures, that over the past few months I've lost the ability to do things calmly, and that I have a councillor waiting for me in a bar in little more than an hour. "You can keep him waiting," he retorts, "it's what you do to everyone else. Maybe I haven't made myself clear: I'm losing patience with you."

The thought of being reprimanded again makes me want to drop everything, to run to the sea and walk on the beach with

Isabelle waiting for the sunset. With her beside me, I could once again see it the way normal people do, watch the sun slowly melting into the waves, the way it does in my sweetest memories. I never thought that one day I'd feel nostalgic for a sunset, just as I never thought I'd get to the point of hating my work and everything it represents, but, despite everything, the ambition that has led me all these years still burns inside me and tells me I mustn't give up, I must do whatever the director asks, once again, as I've always done, until I follow him into his office.

First, it's just an awkward exchange of opinions. Mine don't stand up, any more than anything else that's left of my life. The director, on the other hand, is shrewd, he doesn't hesitate to put the knife in, and he's impatient, the way everyone is now towards me. At the umpteenth question to which he doesn't obtain a prompt response, he throws me a look full of contempt and starts shouting, "This isn't a game here! Don't you realize you owe everything to my support? I trusted you, I treated you like a son! And now I find myself dealing with a completely different man. You don't seem to give a damn about anything any more. Congratulations, you're throwing your future away!"

This time I react as if it isn't the director talking to me, but You, Father Time: "You have no idea of the sacrifices I'm making so as not to throw my future away!"

The director's eyes widen. "Sacrifices? Do you actually have the nerve to call them sacrifices? You don't even realize what you're saying any more. And that's no surprise, given that you can't even seem to think clearly! Just look at your office, it's become a pigsty. And as I always say, someone who can't keep his things tidy can't keep his thoughts tidy."

I can't bear this onslaught any more, it'll end up consuming me. So I decide to turn things round the other way. "It's never

124

happened to you, has it?" I reply. "You've never been in a situation you didn't understand. You're far-sighted, you always see everything with extreme clarity. Even when it's something that reduces a man to having no more time left, like a terminal illness, and yet that same man decides to waste what little time he does have, continuing to work in the same company, the company that's been his whole life."

He turns pale. He's speechless. All at once, he can't think of any more reprimands to fling at me. He takes a few steps back, I think he's suffering from the pathological phobia he has towards any kind of illness. From the way he looks at me, I can guess what illness has just flashed through his mind: Svevo Romano is a womanizer, and he's irresponsible, he probably doesn't take any kind of precautions. Svevo Romano must have AIDS. I can almost see it, that whole tangle of thoughts, that obsession that insinuates itself into the bigoted mechanisms of his mind. He must be wondering if the virus is already everywhere, if I've spread it around the room with my hands. It might be anywhere, lying in wait, ready to get in through the myriad of tiny wounds on his skin. It's on the chair, on his clothes, on the pen he has in his hand, which he immediately puts down on the desk. Everything is contaminated. And his greatest anxiety is: "What's to become of all this? The investments, the worldwide properties? Who'll take care of my empire?" Two ex-wives and a daughter who only calls him to ask for money. I can't see anything else in his mind. How could I ever have wanted to take his place? The master of my life obsessed with the fear of death. The pterodactyl, who moves shrewdly in the circles that matter, surrounded by a herd of eohippuses without prospects, suddenly trapped by his own hang-ups, a mental disorder fed by fear and ignorance.

He keeps his distance. "Svevo," he says, "what's happened to you?"

"Nothing," I reply, going to the door.

"Is there anything you want to tell me?"

"Not today, I have no time to lose." And it's true, Father Time: while You're racing like this, I have no intention of wasting what little time I have left being dependent on him. "I won't be in tomorrow," I inform him, coolly. "I'll see you next week, for the signing of the contract. For anything else, ask Elena."

He's staring at me with revulsion, but I surprise him by retracing my steps, giving him a vigorous handshake and bidding him a formal farewell.

Once out of his office, my time, with its leaps and gaps, again overwhelms me: it's after four, and I'm a quarter of an hour late for my appointment with the councillor.

I get to the restaurant nearly half an hour later.

I ask a waiter, who's busy clearing a table, for information.

"He ordered two coffees and left a while ago. He looked a bit impatient."

What an incredible relief, discovering that for the first time it's a matter of complete indifference to me.

14

M Y APARTMENT ISN'T FAR from the Campo de' Fiori, but I don't know how many hours of common time it would take me to get there on foot. I give the driver a day off and about nine in the morning call a taxi.

I'm in a hurry, but I'm consoled by the thought of seeing her and the magical possibility that everything might slow down again. The closer I get, the tighter the childish knot in my stomach. I glance at my watch: another half-hour has flown by, as imperceptibly as ever. At the end of the Via del Pellegrino, the noisy market appears before me: first of all, the stalls selling fabrics and kitchen utensils. At this hour of the morning it's at its most crowded. It's a hot June day, and the old square, tolerating the stallholders' din, seems to be bursting with life. The smells of the market mingle together: the blasts of hot air from the rotisserie, the odour of newly cooked pizza, the sharp aroma of dripping olives and the sickly scent of the crates of fruit. They wash away my anxiety, and everything gradually returns to its natural rhythm.

"Fresh fruit! Look how soft these grapes are!" The stallholders lavish praise on their produce, holding forth to their little audience. Amid all the people pushing, shouting, asking for things, muttering, I'm searching for her. It only takes a moment before my gaze comes to rest on a point that seems random, but isn't really random at all, and our eyes meet. The confusion, the shouts, everything comes to an abrupt halt. There's nothing else left except her and her flowered skirt. "I was looking for you," I say, as I walk towards her.

"Me too."

Isabelle has just bought some huge lemons, and now she's searching for a grater. Giulia is chattering to herself, alternating vowels and consonants in a language only she can understand. She's happy, she gives me a comical grin, opening her mouth wide and screwing up her little blue eyes with enthusiasm. She doesn't look much like her mother, but she does have the same smile.

As we search for lemon graters, Isabelle asks me if I want to hold Giulia. I don't have time to refuse, I'm already face to face with that little pink bundle.

It's the first time I've ever been so close to a child and I'm surprised to discover that the contact is far from unpleasant, although fraught with anxiety: I'm afraid she'll fall, that she'll slip out of my arms or notice my discomfort. But she stays quite still against my chest, and continues to smile at me. There's no real reason, but she just keeps smiling.

"Oh, here it is, just what I was looking for." Isabelle has finally found her lemon grater. She turns and asks me, "Do you like it?"

It's an ordinary yellow lemon grater, with a transparent plastic cover. But the way she touches it, opens it and examines it makes it seem precious.

"Do you ever come here?"

"Not often, and you?"

"I live just up there." She points to a balcony at the top of a building on the right. "Those geraniums you see are mine."

"Do you live alone?"

"A woman comes a couple of times a week to do the cleaning, the rest of the time there's just me and Giulia."

She's ready to take her daughter in her arms again, and as soon as she takes her off me I realize that I'd like her back. We'd found our own balance.

As we buy bread and slices of pizza, Isabelle tells me which are her favourite shops, the habits she can't live without. About a hundred metres from the square, there's a shop that rents out good films, which is great for her because she's quite a film buff, and it's embarrassing to realize that I'm almost completely ignorant on the subject. When it comes to literature, too, it turns out Isabelle has always been a voracious reader, although she prefers the more intimist kind of novel, and I'd like to be able to enliven the conversation with some interesting quotations but, apart from a few historical or philosophical anecdotes, not much comes to mind. I've spent most of my life with numbers.

She doesn't seem to be bothered by these major differences. She takes me by the hand and gives me a light, infectious smile that seems to be saying: We have plenty of time, we may even discover paths we never thought of exploring before, don't be in a hurry. And with my hand in hers, walking on these black paving stones that smell of life, the sheer everydayness of this little slice of the metropolis has never seemed so invigorating: the restaurant owner coming to the door for a drag on his cigarette, the florist chatting at the side of the street with the waitress from the bar opposite, the market vendors joking among themselves… Everybody seems so relaxed, even a little indolent to me, but of course they know how to take their time. Isabelle greets them,

129

stops to chat, listens to their confidences and keeps receiving gifts: a rose, some basil, a handful of pine nuts for making pesto. The truth is, she knows how to deal with people. She doesn't make distinctions, she treats everybody the same.

We reach the front door of the building where she lives. Inside, there's a little lift, but she keeps walking right past it towards the stairs.

"What floor are you?"

"The fourth."

"What about the lift?"

"I don't trust the lift," she says, and I smile. To think that, of all people, I met a woman like her!

I take Giulia in my arms, and we divide the shopping bags. The stairs are not very inviting: the closer we get to her floor, the steeper they get. After the second flight we hear a dog barking, then a woman yelling "Pablo, stop it!" There's an odour of fried onions and detergent, while the walls smell of the fresh paint someone has crudely applied to it to disguise a small crack.

Isabelle's apartment is much more welcoming than the rest of the building. The dark clay floor and the wooden beams on the ceiling are typical of apartments in the centre, the furnishings are bohemian, the kitchen filled with colourful accessories, and there are piles of books in Italian and French, DVDs and photographs. There's something comforting about all this untidiness, about Giulia's toys scattered everywhere, about the old French books on the shelves, the collections of poetry, the 1960s refrigerator that she's decided to use as a dresser and the antique wrought-iron crib she's transformed into a window box. Timeworn objects given a second life, like shells gathered on the beach and strung onto a necklace or glued to a jewel box. Isabelle also has a passion for buses, Fifties- and Sixties-style buses with rounded corners. She has collected so many objects showing buses, she's lost count. There's a really nice tin clock shaped like a stylized bus just next to the TV set. "Talking of spending your life sitting down," she says as she conscientiously picks up Giulia's toys and puts them in a basket. "The only way to feel you're not missing anything when you travel is to look out of the window. It's like seeing a good film or reading an interesting book. Sometimes it's worth stopping, though, don't you think?"

The way she looks at me, after expressing such a flexible yet resonant idea, is so extraordinarily relevant to what I'm living through, it takes my breath away. In my life I've had to deal with politicians, bankers, people in authority, I used to know how to rattle off clever remarks, obtain favours, box people into corners if necessary, but nobody ever left me speechless. Nobody until today.

Beyond the door of the bedroom, I see a few photographs on the walls and recognize her. She's very young, and wearing a ballerina's tutu. Now I understand where she gets that long straight neck, that elegant bearing. "I used to dance when I was a little girl," she says, when she notices me looking at them. "But it was never very serious."

"So you stopped?"

"I love life too much to let it be taken over by a single passion," she says as she goes into the kitchen to sort out the lunch at the stove: the water for the pasta, the cherry tomatoes for the sauce. Everything about the way she talks and behaves suggests a deep culture, but she's also an old-fashioned, highly organized mother and housewife. She moves with great dexterity in this cluttered space. Here too, there are plenty of photographs, most of them of Giulia: having a bath, at the sea, with a funny hat and a joke pair of glasses. Isabelle stops in front of one of them and with the air of someone who never gets tired of looking at it says, "This

131

is my favourite. There's so much of me in her, in that smile of hers." I also look at it closely, and for a fraction of a second have a feeling I've already lived through this moment. Now we're again looking straight at each other and I want to kiss her. I feel a kind of enthusiasm growing inside me that I've never known, or that I may have forgotten in the disenchantment of all the easy lays I've collected over the years. It's just a kiss, a tender little kiss, where you hold back desire for the sake of something bigger, and yet it's like one's first ever kiss, a completely different way of looking at the world.

I like the taste of her, so different from what I'm accustomed to, and I especially like the fact that when we catch our breaths and look at each other again there isn't the slightest trace of embarrassment between us. It's all so natural, so spontaneous.

In the meantime, Giulia is sitting in her high chair waiting for her baby food. Isabelle goes back to the stove to liquidize some vegetables and the kitchen fills with inviting smells. I sit down next to Giulia. She's exploring the upholstery on the back of her seat with her tiny fingers, while also trying to loosen her belt, but before she can get upset her mother intervenes promptly with a biscuit. Giulia takes it, drags it across the feeding tray so that it crumbles a bit, then lifts it. I don't think she has any intention of eating it, she seems to be wondering what would happen if she dropped it on the floor. After a while, she stops wondering and just drops it. That's the nice thing about children, there are many things in my life I wish I had the courage to deal with the way she's dealt with that biscuit.

Her food is ready, and I ask Isabelle if I can be the one to give it to Giulia. She laughs her head off at my attempts to deal with Giulia's constant moving. I try to persuade the child to eat by imitating a plane, and get a spoonful in the face for my pains.

The spaghetti with fresh pesto and small tomatoes is delicious, and the most surprising thing is that I have all the time I need to savour it. Isabelle doesn't hurry me, just keeps looking at me with that enchanting smile.

When we finish eating, I help her to clear the table. I don't think I've ever cleared a table in my life, and she's amused by my clumsy attempts to hide the fact. As far as I can remember I've never even washed a plate, but Isabelle doesn't have a dishwasher, the one she had is broken and she's never replaced it. "There are a whole lot of things I always forget to do," she says, adding, "I've never been much good with machines." She pours a little detergent in the sink and I offer to help her. She laughs again. "Don't be silly, I can do it myself." But I insist, and find myself sharing the sink and a little sponge with her, earning some more laughter from her.

We put Giulia to bed and sit down on the sofa. I find an open book under the cushion. She starts to tidy it a little, but I stop her with a kiss. I kiss her on the mouth, on the neck, again on the mouth, I'm like a young boy trying to hold in his excitement. I don't have the courage to go further, not because I don't feel the desire, but out of respect, the kind I've never had for any other woman before. Not only is Giulia sleeping in the other room, but given how incredibly slowly time is passing when I'm with Isabelle, there's no urgency. I'm not so crazy as to risk ruining everything.

I look at her: any physical defects I might have noticed the first time I saw her have vanished. The lines around her eyes, the fact that she doesn't have the fresh skin or perfectly firm body of a twenty-year-old, with a round arse and no trace of cellulite, the kind of arse I've always looked for in a woman: none of that matters. Then I don't see her any more, I feel her and that's enough, it all boils down to a matter of skin. And the gentle way she disarms me, the confidence visible in every gesture, the way she confronts life as if it would never end. She surrenders to the passing of time, trying to savour what remains, and simultaneously digging within to know herself better every day. I wonder if it's possible to look someone in the eyes and see all this in such a short time. Isabelle, with her inexplicable ability to slow my life right down, shows me that yes, it is possible.

We interrupt our adolescent kisses to catch our breaths, and lie on the sofa talking, looking up at the ceiling beams, the veins in the wood with their whimsical shapes. Isabelle strokes my hair and tells me about a book she's reading for the third time. She says there are certain masterpieces that should be read several times, life is a constant evolution. Reopening a book that has been important to you can mean setting out on a new journey, perhaps a different one, being able to catch references and meanings that may have escaped you on a first reading. She has a visceral vision of things, the ability to focus only on the present without worrying too much about what has been and what will be. And she makes me feel like that book. If she had leafed through me a few months ago, she might not have been able to read me. I myself have never stopped to read myself, and the paradox of this sudden race against time is that since everything has speeded up, in reality I've stopped running. And even though physically, in these past few months, I've tried to keep up with my own life, my real race began a long time ago. And now that she's stroking my hair, with gentle, circular, soporific movements, it's like stopping for the first time, in every sense. The profound tiredness I've been dragging around with me for too long is gradually overtaken by the deepest sleep I can ever remember.

I sleep all the hours it seems to me I've never slept. A sleep expanding through time, weightless, dreamless, a pure, regenerative sleep. I sleep so well that when I wake up, I forget my name for a moment. Then I see her smiling at me. "I like to watch you sleep," she says.

I realize it's already dark.

"Don't worry, it's only just eight. I've made you something for dinner."

A brief moment of unease. "What about Giulia? I've taken advantage of your kindness, I really should be going."

"Don't be silly... You don't have to be so formal with me. I've put Giulia to bed, and I really want to have dinner with you, if you don't have any other plans. We can eat whenever you like. Are you hungry?"

I ask her if I can take a shower first. She gives me a towel and leads me to the bathroom, which turns out to be the most surprising part of the apartment. The walls, originally white, are almost entirely covered with writing: fragments of songs, passages from novels, thoughts. They have a uniformity of style that gives this fresco a certain artistic refinement. There are a couple of magic markers next to the washbasin, one black and one red. "Don't pay any attention to this nonsense," she says apologetically.

"It's obvious you're someone who wants to leave her mark."

Isabelle smiles and holds out a marker. "Do you want to leave a mark, too?"

"Do you ask everyone who comes into this bathroom the same question?"

"No," she replies, her eyes fixed on mine. "Only the people I trust."

As I go to take the marker, I pull her towards me and kiss her again, with more passion now, my hands glide over her body, I discover her figure for the first time. When my excitement becomes unbearable, I stop, and busy myself with the marker. "One day

I'll write you a nice story," I tell her, putting it down again next to the washbasins. "A story about you and about time passing."

"You've made me curious."

"I'd really like you to become my story."

There's a lovely gleam in her eyes, a surprised smile, her face has filled with happiness, like a child unwrapping presents. She goes out to lay the table, leaving me to my shower.

We're sharing an unexpected, perhaps premature intimacy, but it's so pleasant to imagine myself an integral part of her life, to leave the bathroom and find her with two glasses of Martini in her hand, ready for a toast. We kiss again, this time only a thin towel separates me from her body and it's more difficult to hide my excitement. I don't think I've ever kissed a woman for such a long time without undressing her first.

This time we eat in the living room, by candlelight. The table is elegantly laid, the menu is a simple one: meatballs in sauce. I can't remember the last time I ate meatballs. They're delicious, every bite arouses an age-old memory. She cooked them while I was asleep, she says they didn't take long, she's used to making this kind of thing.

There's a certain freedom in the way our lives are so different, but at the same time Isabelle makes me want to start all over again, to wipe out my errors, to ignore my sins. It's easier to hide with people we care about. We're capable of telling the darkest aspects of our existence to a perfect stranger but when we're with people who mean a lot to us we keep our secrets, we don't want even to imagine what they might think of us if they discovered them.

We both want to make love, the desire for it fairly oozes from our eyes, but for the first time I know what it means to want to wait, to be afraid that I'm not ready.

After dinner we say goodbye at the door. Once again her kisses and hugs tell me: Stay, I want you inside me, all night long. But I'm afraid that part of her may feel uncomfortable in the cold light of day, and I'm trying to respect her.

"Tomorrow Giulia's daddy is coming to pick her up to spend the weekend with her," she says, holding me tightly in her arms.

I invite her to have dinner out. "I'm looking forward to tomorrow," I add, knowing that as soon as I've walked out through the door of this apartment, my time, inexplicably, will start racing again.

15

WHEN I'M NOT WITH HER You sweep me away. I have to be firm, keep my thoughts at bay, the anxiety which again envelops everything like a thick icy fog. Like a scene from a bad film, I constantly replay the image of the director, looking at me with that scared expression, as if I was a plague victim to be kept at a distance. As soon as I move away from that oasis of peace which is her life, my responsibilities, my conditioning, everything to do with my life as I've thought of it up until now, begins to tire me. I'm screwing everything up, and I still can't quite accept the idea of throwing away years of sacrifice.

Luckily there are the messages, the phone calls, all those words that fill the time until dinner. Words coloured with enthusiasm, with the desire to seduce. Words that bring relief.

I pick her up in my car. I arrive a few minutes late, but she's waiting for me outside her building with an indulgent smile. At last I can catch my breath.

I've booked a table in a top-class restaurant. I know the owner, and he greets us at the door with a great deal of flattery. Isabelle moves casually through the beautifully furnished room, defusing all my usual weapons of seduction: she doesn't seem the slightest bit impressed by the surroundings, any more than she was impressed earlier, in the car, when I pressed my foot on the accelerator with my usual smugness. From time to time I get the feeling she's tense. Even when we toast, with a vintage champagne that'll cost me a fortune, she seems uneasy. And when she places a hand on my arm, with an almost childlike gentleness, I suddenly understand. I'm the one who's tense and unnatural. I'm expecting the most from all this impeccable elegance without it really being necessary, and my anxiety has spread throughout the restaurant, affecting the other customers and the waiters. I realize that it's the first time in I don't know how long that I've come to a place like this without any cocaine in my system. But then she strokes my wrist, and I relax, like a child. I look deep into her eyes, and the rest ceases to matter.

I'd like to be able to tell her about my life, the things I'm not proud about, my weaknesses, especially the incredible adventure I'm living through. But I fear her judgement, I'm afraid of losing her. Can you tell a woman, especially on a first date, that your own time has gone mad? That you've been flung into a new dimension, where things and people sometimes get distorted, get old in front of your eyes, due to some kind of hallucination, and that perhaps part of the blame is down to the drugs you've overindulged in and all the other uninhibited aspects of a modern lifestyle? All-encompassing though her smile may be, I doubt there is room in it for all that.

I'm a bit less evasive about my childhood and my strange relationship with my family. I tell her about my mother's death, and for the first time I manage to talk about it openly, without filters imposed by circumstances, like a child free to draw on a blank sheet. I'm encouraged by the totally natural empathy in her eyes when I describe my claustrophobic years at boarding school and the more carefree ones at university in England, or when I tell her how impossible it is for me to go back to my roots.

"I certainly would never have guessed you're Piedmontese," she says at a certain point. "You don't have a trace of an accent."

"To be honest, I've never felt Roman either."

"But there must be somewhere in the world where you feel at home."

"Nowhere in particular," I confess. "Though last year I went to Tuscany, a really beautiful spot in Tuscany, where the countryside has something magical about it, and I suddenly decided to buy a house in the area. I'm currently renovating it. It used to be a monastery, and it's really lovely. That's somewhere I think I might actually feel at home."

As I talk to Isabelle, not far from our table I spot my old friend the Deputy, having dinner with his wife. Our eyes meet and I feel myself turn pale. The last time we saw each other, we were cocooned in the pleasant atmosphere of an evening he thought was private, an evening full of slaps on the back, confidences, friendly smiles, which the director then used for his own ends, and now his eyes are burning with fear and resentment and he looks as if he'd like to beat me to a pulp.

When I pay the bill and we get up from the table to leave the restaurant, the Deputy approaches me. Addressing a forced smile to Isabelle, he takes me to one side. "You should be ashamed of what you stand for," he says in a voice that's barely audible but as taut as a violin string, discreetly sinking his nails into my arm. "You think you have me by the balls. I may have some weaknesses, but I'd never be capable of stooping to your level."

Then he turns away and walks back to his table.

Isabelle is looking at me. "He's a politician, isn't he? I've seen him on television."

I nod, taking her by the hand and leaving the restaurant with her. I can't hide the sense of unease his words have left me with. In the car, she strokes my forehead, and gives me what's intended to be a reassuring smile.

The unease grows even more once we've entered my apartment. Isabelle looks around, but without the amazed reaction the women who've set foot in here before her have accustomed me to. No ecstatic smile, no open-mouthed gaping at all the hi-tech gadgetry. The only thing that seems to delight her is the view from the window of the living room, though she does glance briefly at the Bonalumi in the dining room, though not so much as to make it seem like one of the more interesting paintings.

I'm sure she recognizes the uniqueness of the apartment in itself, but I fear that the cold, minimalist style of decoration makes her uncomfortable.

And the fact that there are no books is hardly a point in my favour either. My designer hadn't seen the need for a bookcase, and what space there is contains just a handful of rather bulky photographic books, and a few others about interior design and the world's top hotels. When Isabelle starts leafing through one of them, with a slightly wary look in her eyes, I go to her and kiss her on the mouth. And suddenly there are no more deputies or architects or not-very-complimentary thoughts about my life. There is only her body, which I carry in my arms to the bedroom and undress with a hitherto concealed urgency, as if it was a secret, a priceless pearl. There are her hands, modestly covering her maternal breasts, and mine, which have only one purpose: to give her pleasure. She is the centre of my interest, the receptacle of everything good. This bed has seen perfect, gorgeous women, but with her, for the first time, I'm surprised by a sense of inadequacy, which I overcome only by giving myself

142

completely, with a dedication I've never known before, until I disappear. I no longer exist. I let myself be annihilated by her slow dance above me, while time dissolves. I am her breath, her moods, her pleasure. As I'm about to come, I withdraw, even though she moans to have me back inside her. And I do it so that I can have my excitement at my disposal for as long as I need. We are like two orphans in an air raid, defenceless and at the same time indestructible. Held tight in her arms, wretched as I am in comparison with Your disarming power, I'm not afraid of You any more. All this might come to an end, there might be nothing but oblivion awaiting me beyond this bed, but I'm inside her, I'm part of her, and not even oblivion scares me any more.

We spend two days like this, never leaving the bed except to go to the bathroom or to have something to eat, like two wild animals, from whatever we find in the refrigerator. Two days which in my time have expanded to an indefinable length. I feel like one of Ulysses' companions, forgetting my identity, drugged with pleasure, at the banquet of the sorceress Circe. We watch a film, we make love, we talk, and we start all over again.

At a certain point, breaking into the idyll of this suspended time without coordinates or directions, a thought crosses my mind. One of those thoughts that seem absurd, nonsensical, until they insinuate themselves into your rational perception of things with such force as to demolish it: what if even this image of the two of us, lying abandoned on this bed, was a hallucination? What if Isabelle wasn't real, or—worse still—what if she wasn't even possible?

"It may seem illogical to you," I say to her without warning, "but I have the feeling you may last for ever and at the same time never have happened."

Isabelle smiles in that reassuring way of hers, and snuggles closer to me, placing her head on my chest. "I'm a mess, really," she confesses, drawing little circles on my skin with her forefinger and thumb together. "With a little child, in a foreign country. Sometimes I think my life has been a long series of mistakes, but I assure you that I really am here. There's only one thing I hope: not to make any more mistakes. I have happened, oh yes, I can swear that I have happened, and I hope to happen for a lot longer."

"I like the way you say things."

"I like the way *you* say things. For ever and never, I think those were the final words of a love letter in *Mauvais sang* by Leos Carax, a film that's been almost completely forgotten. Love can be so overwhelming, it stays inside you for ever, even if you've never experienced it."

I stroke her hair and look at her, thinking of all the men she has loved before she met me, maybe that long series of mistakes she spoke about a moment ago, and I feel a pang in the pit of my stomach, a sensation I've never felt before. I assume it's jealousy, the kind of jealousy that may even become intolerable. "Have you ever known that?" I ask her. "A love for ever and never?"

Isabelle pulls a face that puts everything back in perspective, even my jealousy. "I don't like leaving things unresolved," she says. "And I feel relatively at peace with my own conscience. If there were accounts to settle, I've settled them. Nobody has stayed inside me like that."

I think about things unresolved in my own life, festering wounds. They have nothing to do with love, at least not with love as she means it. They look like my father and sound like all the words I've never been able to say to him.

"What about you? Have you ever known a love that was for ever and never?"

She wouldn't believe me—she might even think me ridiculous—if I told her I've never been in love. So I just smile at her, a shy smile, to which she responds with an amused pout, like a little girl. "I'm always the one to reveal myself, but never mind." She gets out of bed to fetch a glass of water, wrapping herself in the sheet as she does so: now I'm the one revealed.

"I don't think so," I say, pulling on the sheet to undress her.

Naked now, Isabelle tries modestly to cover herself with her hands. "I feel embarrassed," she says, coming back to the bed to take possession of the sheet again.

She's turned red. Suddenly overwhelmed by tenderness, I take her face in the palm of my hand. I'm surprised by such girlish modesty in a woman like her.

She confesses that it's the first time since she had Giulia that she's slept with a man. For her, this beautiful interlude in my bed has the fresh taste of rebirth and the bitter taste of guilt. For more than a year her body has been a cradle, transforming itself to welcome a new life. She tells me that in the first few days after Giulia was born, she would look in the mirror and wonder if sex would ever again be part of her life. The last time before that had been the bored, mechanical act of a Sunday afternoon, a clear symptom of the fact that, after almost ten years of living together, she and Giulia's father had reached the end of the line, and yet it led, mysteriously, to conception. Even from the final stages of a love affair, something much bigger can come, overcoming everything, even death.

Again that pang in the pit of my stomach. I imagine that sharing in the conception of a new life is a gesture of absolute, unforgettable love, even for two people who are barely on speaking terms. A gesture which is like a bond, something set in concrete.

I stroke her stomach, that soft, maternal stomach, which she keeps hiding from my gaze, and touch her belly button with one finger. She smiles, I keep pressing with my finger, as if the belly button was a hole in a balloon and I was afraid that she might deflate at any moment and fly away. Then I tell her that she's mine, mine and nobody else's.

"People aren't like apartments or cars," she answers, with a distant smile. "You can't own people."

"But I feel that I'm yours," I tell her, trying to keep my tone light, however serious the words. "You could do anything you like with me."

"I'd never put a label on you, like those people who tattoo their bodies with names and dates... That's always disgusted me."

"Well, then I disgust you too," I continue, still lightly. "Tomorrow I'm going to have your name tattooed on my chest in capital letters. Or rather no, you know what I'm going to do? I'm going to have my whole body covered with your initials. I'm yours! I want to shout it to the whole world!"

She bursts out laughing. "Stop it! I'm sure you'd even be scared of one of my magic markers," she says, reaching out her hand to her bag, which is under the bedside table. She takes out one of the markers I saw in her bathroom, her face like a naughty child's. "Want to bet?"

"You really are obsessed!" I say, with a laugh. "Don't tell me you were intending to scribble all over my apartment."

She approaches me, brandishing the marker threateningly. "Didn't you just tell me you wanted to have my name tattooed all over your body?"

"And didn't you just tell me you were against possession and would never put a label on me?"

We start fighting, like two little children. We tickle each other, we laugh, we laugh until we can't breathe, ending up looking each other in the eyes, motionless, and at the same time wanting to go beyond those eyes. I'd like to penetrate the most inaccessible cavities of her mind.

Isabelle is the first to look away. "Come on, let me write something on your body! You said I could do anything I wanted with you, and now you're scared of a few measly words!"

I surrender. She makes me turn on my stomach and sits astride me. "Do you want me to scribble on your back?" I feel the cold tip of the marker on my neck.

"But if you do it there I'll never be able to read what you write!"

"That's the best part of it!" she replies, moving her marker without my being able to see anything.

"That's enough now," I say, leaping up suddenly, and again I rugby-tackle her, simulating the noises of a maddened animal. I hold her tight, while she struggles, still laughing. We end up making love once again. It's better every time. We settle into it, and it's so simple, the way we move, the way we give each other pleasure. Finally, sated and satisfied, we lie in each other's arms, two twins in their mother's womb, and stay like that, suspended, for all the time we need.

In the middle of this tranquil oblivion, all at once she breaks the silence: "I have to call Giulia's father, I'm an awful mother."

"You're wonderful," I reassure her. And I really do think that as she talks on the telephone to her little girl, whispering tender promises to her.

"I have to pick her up tomorrow morning at eight," she says after hanging up. "Do you realize how much time we've spent here? It's Sunday."

147

The first reference to time since we sank onto this bed. If it wasn't for her, I wouldn't even know what time it is, which month we're in, and I don't even care.

"I'm hungry, and we've emptied the fridge."

"Do you want to go out?"

"No…" she moans, stretching. "I'd be fine with a pizza."

"There's a place just near here, I can go down and get something. Will you wait for me here?"

I grab a tracksuit from the wardrobe. I feel completely devoid of strength, I'd never go out if it wasn't a matter of life and death.

She laughs and sticks her head under the pillow. "Let's enjoy this last night," she says, her voice muffled. I leave the room, thinking I don't like the word *last*.

As I go down in the lift, then walk along the street, then go into the restaurant and order the pizzas, then sit at a table waiting for them, all I keep doing is smelling my hands, lingering over her perfume to convince myself she exists. She's waiting for me in my apartment, I tell myself.

When I get back, noisily closing the door behind me, the first thing that surprises me is the unnatural silence of the apartment, then the distinct thought that I'll go into the bedroom and realize she isn't there, that she's melted like a vision.

What I can't imagine is that, beyond that door, something even worse is waiting for me.

The shelf under the bedside table has been raised. I suddenly realize that I never got rid of that bag of cocaine. Isabelle has it in her hands now. She's standing there, completely naked, but she looks distracted, as if her mind is suddenly miles away.

"I can explain—"

Her eyes stop me dead. She drops the cocaine on the ground. I do the same with the pizzas.

"You're an addict," she says, looking at me in dismay.

"It isn't mine."

"You're an addict," she repeats. "No, you're more than that... Nobody keeps a quantity like that in their home if they're not..."

"Are you joking? Don't even think it."

"What is it, then?"

"I told you, it isn't mine."

She looks me straight in the eyes. She's weighing up my lie, and she's doing it with a surgical coldness.

Then she looks away and starts searching for her clothes. "I have a little child," she says as she puts her skirt on. "As long as she's with me she'll never know that stuff like this even exists."

I stand there without saying a word, crushed by the weight of my own weakness, gathered there in that plastic bag.

I know that something irreparable has just happened. Isabelle is walking out of my life and I don't open my mouth, I don't lift a finger to stop her. When she finishes dressing, she picks up her handbag and walks past me without even looking me in the face. At the noise of the door closing, I feel anxiety growing inside me.

I know, You've started racing again.

I clench my fists in order not to scream, I restrain myself from destroying everything within reach. What I do attack is that plastic bag, that insignificant relic of a distant life. I never had the courage to show myself to Isabelle for what I am: another relic, like everything around me.

The powder flies up when I hit the bag. I blow it, angrily. The world can't go any faster than this. The only thing worse than this is death.

But then I'm forced to change my mind. I turn to the window and see the sun, looking as if it's wrapped in ash-grey steam, emerging from between the buildings at breakneck speed. I collapse on the bed, devoid of strength. I think of the length of my existence, the way my heart thumps when she takes my face in her hands, our breathing, so deep that it seems to fill the entire space, then I think of the age of the sun and stars, and suddenly I see them shrink in a flash, just a fluttering of wings in the immensity of the universe, and almost involuntarily I find myself bowing my head before Your omnipotence.

16

I DON'T GET OUT OF BED for two days. She hasn't been in touch, and when I call her she doesn't answer the phone. The only person still looking for me is Elena, my secretary, and she's paid to do it. On the screen of my mobile I even find a call from my father, from a few days ago. He's left me a message saying that he's tried to contact me several times and that we have to speak, if he could he'd even come and see me himself, but he's been saying that more or less since he brought me into the world. Then again that silence, I can sense the pride in it, even over the phone. "End of messages," the electronic voice informs me. I can still remember when my voicemail was overflowing with requests, appointments, greetings. You just have to remove yourself from the flow to realize you're not indispensable, quite the contrary. I have to find my way again, think up a plan to raise myself out of this abyss.

I get up. I don't even look at myself in the mirror. I put on a pair of trousers, a jacket, and go out. I have to find her again, and discover what the hell I can do to slow down my life.

I go back to the Campo de' Fiori. The market seems more chaotic than when I saw it with her. I rush through it to her front door.

I press the button by the entryphone. I don't know how long I stand there waiting for an answer, a woman's voice saying "Come up". But there's nothing.

Elena keeps calling me on my mobile, the way my time is racing makes her seem even more persistent. I have to switch the phone off before the ringing perforates my brain.

It's colder today than it was a few days ago. Clouds heavy with rain are moving quickly to obscure the last slivers of sky. They're racing, but not a breath of wind is blowing.

Maybe Isabelle is here somewhere, hidden amid the crowd in the market. She may even have passed close to me, with Giulia in her arms, and in the speed of the moment I didn't even notice. With every step I take to look for her, another few minutes go by, flying up like splinters out of control. The confusion sets my heart pounding. I can hear my heartbeats everywhere, in my ears, my muscles, my bones. The voices merge in my head, until they become ever more cacophonous and incomprehensible. "That street there. What size? The biggest, thanks. Was it really the day before yesterday? Ten, thanks. There aren't any cherry tomatoes... Which pasta? No, the pizza. How many kilometres? I told him I... My father would like to see... How old? I haven't set foot... There must be one... In what context?... To lunch. I'm not there. I wouldn't be able... How many? That moon. A piano. A pound of bananas... Onion. There are ten... Here. Pasta. Butter. Kitchen... I'm..." Enough! I put my hands over my ears, I can't stand it any more. I can't stand the noise of the crowd when time is racing like this.

I'd like to get down on my knees, to surrender, to beg for mercy, to know what I've done to deserve all this. But I stand there, stiff-backed, my feet solidly planted on the paving stones. You'll never destroy me.

I don't know what time it is, but I know it's late, because suddenly the crowd disperses, the van doors are closed, the square empties.

The sky has grown darker. Soon, in fact very soon, it'll start to rain. I zip up my jacket and raise the collar. It's damp, and the cold penetrates my bones like the sharp nails of an old witch. Then the first drops of rain start to fall, heavy and fast. The black sky, shaken by constant rumbling, is stormy and fascinating. For a few minutes the rain comes down with unusual intensity. And I stand alone in the middle of the square and raise my face to the sky in an act of defiance. I want to feel the force of that rain on my face, I want to be struck and scarred by Your anger.

I can't manage by myself. I need to see her again, I have to find a way to make it up with her. I go to a bar on the square to wait for my clothes to dry out. I must look terrible, I can see it in people's eyes.

I keep phoning her, but she never answers. In the end I decide to call Luca, our only mutual acquaintance, the only bridge still standing between us.

He answers.

He sounds a bit wary, although he doesn't seem to know what's been going on. "I'm sorry I haven't been in touch," he says. "I've been very busy."

What he means is that he didn't like the idea of helping me with Isabelle, but now doesn't seem the time to point that out, it would be a waste of breath. Besides, I need to be friends with him again, I need to gain his trust and get him to arrange a dinner, an excursion, anything. "It's been a difficult time," I say. "Getting out of the scene… You know what I mean, I can talk to you because I know you understand. How about meeting for a coffee, or maybe we can have dinner one of these evenings..."

Immediately his attitude changes. "I can tell from your voice that you're not well," he says sadly. "We could have met tonight, but it's Giorgio's birthday and we're going to the Prime." He pauses for a moment, and when he starts speaking again I get the feeling he's smiling. "I'd ask you to join us, but the last time you weren't very friendly to him."

I smile, too. As far as I'm concerned, the fact that it's Giorgio's birthday this evening and that he may also have invited Isabelle suits me down to the ground. "The Prime? I didn't think you still liked places like that."

"Just because I left that whole scene doesn't mean I only go to out-of-town restaurants," he replies, amused, but he's in a hurry to say goodbye. God alone knows how many precious minutes I've made him waste.

When I hang up, Elena calls me again. I have no time for the hassles of work, outside it's already dark. I manage to get in a taxi and rush to the restaurant. If all goes well, I might get there by the time they're having dessert.

The last time I set foot in this place, Gaëlle was in Rome. She and I and Federico had booked a table at the back, the most isolated. Thinking back on that evening now, I can imagine the two of them seeking out each other's hands when I wasn't looking.

The people here are the ones I've known for years, have spent endless evenings with. They say hello, a little surprised, some ask what's become of me, others ask me, "Everything all right?" My clothes are still wet, and I probably look a bit suspicious.

There's also the risk I might run into Federico. Wednesday's a busy night, they might have booked a table in one of these rooms. I realize it doesn't bother me. This evening I'm here for her. I want to look her in the eye and take her away with me.

Obviously I'm not really ready to see her again. When her beautiful freckled face appears in my field of vision, I immediately freeze.

That Giorgio is talking into her ear. I doubt it's anything amusing, but she's smiling. Not very naturally, of course, but she is smiling. Then he pours a little wine in her glass and Isabelle pretends to be flattered, which doesn't suit her at all. When she turns in my direction, maybe responding to the appeal in my eyes, she abruptly changes expression.

I'd like to get into her head, now that I'm doing the round of the tables, greeting people without taking my eyes off her, not even for a moment, I'd like to be able to feel what she's feeling, know if she too, like me, is trembling inside.

Luca is surprised, but greets me in a friendly manner. We exchange knowing glances, he must have assumed I'd put in an appearance, deep down I'm still the same Svevo, the one who never gives up.

Isabelle gets to her feet, saying she has to go to the toilet, and I immediately follow her.

She realizes I'm behind her and she keeps moving quickly along the corridor. A waitress in a kimono gets in my way. "Isabelle, please," I cry, but she doesn't slow down.

When she gets to the door she turns, and her eyes tell me to leave her alone. But I don't give up. I follow her into the Ladies.

A couple of girls are fixing their make-up in front of the mirror. Seeing me, they turn as pale as the powder puffs in their hands.

"Can I talk to you?"

"To say what?"

"Not here."

She's agitated, she begs me to leave.

"So that you can go back to the table with that man?"

Our two spectators have got their colour back and walk out without saying anything, leaving us alone.

"His name is Giorgio, he's a good man."

"Please, listen to me. Let me at least explain."

"Explain then, but hurry up about it."

I thought it would be easier, that the magic of what we've been through together would soften her. But time is still racing, it won't slow down, and Isabelle is just as impatient with me as everyone else is. She doesn't give me time to speak.

"They warned me about you," she says, turning her back on me. "I don't want to fall for it, I can't afford to. We're too different. Please go away."

I go to her and grab her by the elbow. At last I smell her perfume, hear her breathing. I'd like to be able to kiss her once again. "You can't believe what people say. That's not like you."

Isabelle is upset, impatient. "I believe what I saw," she says, walking away. "And it's not for me. Leave me alone, please."

"I can't. You're in my blood."

The door of one of the cubicles opens, and who should come out but Gaëlle, her sinuous body held tightly in a black sheath dress. "Svevo," she calls to me. She looks surprised and annoyed.

Isabelle takes the opportunity to leave.

I don't have time to stop her, because Gaëlle has already come and stood in front of me. "Have you been reduced to following women into the ladies' toilet?" she says in that haughty tone of hers.

"The kind of place you shouldn't even set foot in," I say, taking out all my anger on her as I try to leave.

But she grabs me again. "Are you trying to tell me I'm not a lady?"

"A lady doesn't use the toilet to do what you do." I don't have time to try and disguise my disgust.

Gaëlle grabs me by the wrist. "Wait."

"What do you want? You should be in Paris."

"Who is that woman?"

"That's none of your business."

"I need to talk to you," she insists.

"We have nothing else to say to each other."

"Do you know why I'm still in Rome?"

Her eyes are soft, yielding, a long way from her usual demeanour. She's beautiful, but decadent, like one of those expensive designer objects that go out of fashion after a while and end up forgotten in some old warehouse. I'm not interested in what she has to tell me. I finally manage to free myself from her grasp and leave the toilet. I'm deaf to her calls. I have to find Isabelle.

As I walk back along the corridor, I see, in an adjacent room, Federico and some of my old friends having dinner, surrounded by glasses of vodka and attractive women. When they see me they fall silent. Federico is embarrassed, he stands up and comes towards me. I feel as if I've never really seen him before now: he's so drunk, he can barely keep on his feet.

"Svevo, listen, I… I think we ought to talk…"

I don't know what comes over me. My arm moves of its own accord. To everyone's amazement, I land him a punch that sends him crashing into one of the nearby tables. A plate of steamed vegetables ends up on his head, like a hat, and the woman who was eating it finds Federico lying at her feet.

SIMONA SPARACO

The punch has attracted attention. In an instant, we're surrounded by curious faces. Among them I see Isabelle. She looks really dejected. Giorgio is behind her. He puts a hand on her shoulder and together they walk away and disappear from my sight.

A couple of young men intervene to hold me back, but there's no need: I've already vented my anger, and Federico doesn't seem in any fit state to retaliate.

At a certain point I realize I'm not the only one staring at him mercilessly. Gaëlle is standing beside me, and there's something diabolical and pleased in her expression.

The manager, who knows me, asks me to leave the restaurant, and he doesn't have to insist, because I want to get out of this place as soon as possible. Maybe Luca was right, Isabelle deserves better.

A moment before getting in the taxi, I turn and see Gaëlle in the entrance. I knew she would follow me.

She reaches me in the twinkling of an eye and says, "Federico's your friend. It's all my fault."

I don't know what role she's playing, or what her next move is, I only know that that punch wasn't only for Federico. It was for all the sordid reasons that kept us together until a short time ago.

"Leave it alone, Gaëlle," I reply, opening the door.

From the window of the moving car I see her rearranging her hair in front of the door, then, in a moment, she is again swallowed up by the fashionable riff-raff still proliferating behind me. Simultaneously, the telephone starts ringing.

It's Elena again. I have to answer.

"It's your father."

I don't even have time to think of an excuse.

"I'm sorry, Signor Romano. He's had a heart attack."

158

17

THERE'S NOTHING SO HUMILIATING as arriving late to your own father's funeral.

I missed the first plane, the one I managed to catch landed on time, but the taxi ride ate up two hours. I wasn't worried until we drew up outside the church and I saw my cousins, who have suddenly become adults, carrying the mahogany coffin down the steps to the hearse.

Although I may have spent the night awake repeating it to myself, it still hasn't sunk in, and now I'm barricading myself behind the absurd belief that it isn't his body inside that coffin, that at any moment he'll come up behind me and say in his usual resentful tone, "Finally made it, eh?"

I can't feel my legs or my hands any more. I walk, but I don't feel anything, just a slight sensation of pins and needles. As if I'm dreaming. I recognize a lot of people, some of whom I haven't seen since I was a child: grey hair, lined faces, serious and composed for the occasion. Dark glasses, vague suggestions of smiles. They are still all here, as if in some way life in this city has been waiting for me. No revolutions, no disasters. Everything is more or less as I left it. Except those who have grown up until they have become other people: my cousin gives me such a tight hug he takes my breath away. My aunt, on the other hand, is more distant. Her eyes are hard, like a reprimand, not so much for what I've done, for my unjustifiable delay, as for what I should have done. And she has my mother's eyes.

"It would have been difficult to put off the funeral until tomorrow," she says as she gets in the car. "I'm sorry you didn't get the opportunity to see him one last time. We'll talk at the cemetery, are you following us?"

Predictably, I lose them on the way and by the time I arrive the coffin has practically already been buried. My aunt looks at me with a resigned air and raised eyebrows.

I approach the grave with the detachment of someone who just happened to be in the area. Obviously there are no names, dates or photographs yet, and as far as I'm concerned, there could be anybody in there.

"Do you remember Anna? Your father's colleague."

A little woman, hidden behind a pair of glasses that are bigger than her, greets me with a hug. "We met the last time you came."

I nod, returning her embrace. "A couple of years ago."

"Nearly seven, actually," my aunt corrects me, with a slight shake of the head.

On the ride home, the grief at last hits me. More than grief, a sense of powerlessness at the thought that he really isn't here any more. It's like punching the wind, a rage that finds no outlet. It will backfire on me. And in fact, the first blow soon surprises me, it comes straight to the pit of my stomach and takes my breath away, so that I have to stop on the road, even though I know that this means keeping my relatives, who must be at my father's apartment by now, waiting even longer.

I get out of the car and vomit. All that comes out is water. It gushes out of me, until the cramp puts a stop to it. The sky is clear, one of those smiling skies that Turin manages to come up with every now and again, the mountains can be seen on the horizon and the air is fresh. I allow myself just a few mouthfuls of it, then get back in the car and set off again.

It's Anna who opens the door to me. She has taken her glasses off and her red, swollen eyes tell me she's been crying continuously and may start again at any moment.

My first impression—that everything in this city is just the way it was—is belied by my father's apartment. There's something different, not so much in the furnishings, as in the photographs, in the colours. It's alive. It's the home of a dead man, but it's alive.

I haven't been to see him for seven years. Seven years. In my head only a couple, at most. I wonder when it was that my perception of time really started to become distorted.

My relatives are talking among themselves, they share moments, memories. I'm not here. I'm cut out. They long ago stopped waiting for me.

When Anna and my aunt tell me about all the bureaucratic formalities I'll need to deal with, I lose the thread of what they're saying. Just one thing hits me in the face, like a slap: "Your father had been ill for months," my aunt says. "He wanted to tell you, it was the thing that mattered most to him. And then, just when he seemed to be responding to the treatment, he had his attack."

I barely have time to recover when I receive another blow, an even more violent one. "He left you a trust," Anna says, taking me aside. "It's a lot of money, more than he could really afford. He made sacrifices all his life to put it aside for you. I know you don't need it, he was so proud of you, and your professional

161

success. But he also said that you were his greatest sorrow. He was always very worried about you."

"How long are you stopping?" my aunt asks, her bag already over her shoulder.

"I have to leave tomorrow, I have an important meeting. But I'll come back soon."

She raises her eyebrows again, but doesn't say anything. Soon afterwards the house rapidly empties. Once I'm alone, surrounded by half-empty wine glasses and extinguished cigarettes, all I can think about is that worry he never expressed, all those cowardly bank transfers which seemed like some kind of solution at the time. Then the excruciating feeling of remorse at the fact that I was never able to talk to him, not even once, about anything, that all I ever did was put things off, thinking that maybe one day… Without realizing that I was filling my life with postponements. With so many unforgivable *not nows*.

I look at him there, posing in the last photographs, framed in the old way. He doesn't even seem to be the same person: a calmer man, a man at peace with his conscience. Only now do I realize that in his way he was trying to break through the wall of ill feeling that had built up between us. I can't say he didn't try. In his own way, of course, but I can't say he didn't do it.

How could I have imagined an outcome like this? Standing here alone in the apartment where my father lived, the man whose love, respect and understanding I kept looking for all through my childhood. A man overwhelmed with grief and inadequate to the role that had descended on him without warning. And now that he's no longer here, everything appears so different. Around my stooped exhausted body, a line of photographs. Of course, I'm in some of them: the day of my graduation, a few birthdays or family meals. I always look so absent, many of those occasions

I don't even remember. I was looking at the camera, but I was looking somewhere else, looking ahead to what I still had to do, to all those things that would have to fill my little days. And then, seven years pass, like a flash, and he goes, without my even giving him time to tell me. The last thing he wanted to tell me is all in those silences, in the heavy breathing that fills the last messages in my voicemail. Now, unexpectedly, he smiles to me from these photographs, and among these objects, tidily collected over the years, I discover something more about his life: the journeys he took, the money he put aside, without ever telling me that he never did anything with the money I sent him. Maybe he was too embarrassed. Or maybe he was just trying to humour me. In his study, there's a wall covered in papers, notes, photographs. My father wrote thoughts, read novels, had a companion. I would never have imagined it. There's a photograph showing him together with Anna in Guatemala. The wind is blowing hard, they are smiling and holding hands. Anna seems about to fly away. Behind them, a stormy sea, a wave almost a couple of metres high is about to crash on the beach. On the back of the photograph, a pencilled note:

Do you remember, Anna? The power of those waves and what the locals used to say: you can't beat the wave. To survive you have to stop. Look it in the face and abandon yourself to its force. That's the only way you hope to save yourself. Salvation is inside you.

I turn the photograph over again and take another look at his smile.

His life is all here, among these papers. He may be gone, but everything is still in its place, and this apartment, like Anna's tears, tell me about him, about the marks he left in time.

My apartment, on the other hand, wouldn't say anything to those left behind. It's a shop window, the work of a brilliant designer. Spotless and antiseptic. A shrine to efficiency and technology. Efficient, above all, at cataloguing parties, tits, arses, fucks. All the same. Perfect bodies, Botoxed, plastic, racing against time, but all the same. My life has been nothing but a long sequence of moments, all of them the same. An hour or a minute, it doesn't matter. How much time wasted, sitting behind a table, spending money or accumulating things which, when the day comes, will all be left behind. I open the desk drawer and there I find my mother, her dark unruly curls, held in place by a gaudy yellow clip. In some photographs I'm with her: those endless afternoons by the sea, playing under the beach umbrella. My mother reading a novel, my father leafing through the newspaper with one hand and stroking her hair with the other. In these photographs, I look at the camera without thinking about what I will be in twenty years. I'm smiling at whoever is taking the photograph, with my hand held tightly in my mother's and the little plastic bucket filled with sand. My fears are small ones, of monsters that don't exist, life itself does not scare me.

I collapse on the bed, and am overcome by the unmistakable smell of tobacco and the aftershave my father used for more than twenty years. I imagine I still have that look, the one I had as a child, and that I'm not afraid, I don't fear the passing of time.

When you're a child everything seems to go so slowly. Feeding all our needs is that love in its pure state, without compromises. That's the kingdom of childhood, where everything is exaggerated, suspended, without coordinates or directions. Happiness is there, in that unmeasured time, in that hand guiding you, in the smell of her skin, which, when life starts racing, you somehow end up forgetting.

18

T HERE COMES A MOMENT when we have to come to terms with what we have been, what we are and what we hope to become. There comes a moment when it is necessary to try to make peace with our own failures, and to dig down into the sometimes nauseating magma of our own consciousness in search of answers. I mustn't erase anything. It isn't too late, I can still start all over again.

This afternoon, the top brass are meeting to sign the long-awaited contract that will give us control of Righini's company, on which the director set his eyes last year. And this very morning, when the agreement gets his signature, I will no longer be formally part of his team, because I've decided to hand in my resignation.

No elegant suit and matching tie for me, I've deliberately opted for a T-shirt and a tracksuit top that I found in my father's wardrobe, still impregnated with his smell. Even though I'm still running, still trying to keep up with You, I at least need to feel comfortable, and the absurd fantasy that I can still feel him near somehow gives me a sense of security.

To tell the truth, my last race was the one at the airport, because I knew the plane wouldn't wait for me. As for the rest, I want to respect my time, and everyone else has to adapt. I have already done enough running.

Antonio is waiting for me when I leave the airport, with his usual disapproving look, the look of someone who's tired of waiting. Not that there's any reason: the plane arrived on time, Signor Romano has no luggage to reclaim, why the hell is he taking so long?

When I get in the car, I tell him that there's no need to go fast, I'm not in any hurry. He seems surprised: maybe he thinks I'm still overcome with grief.

I am, but discreetly, it doesn't show through in any way, it's just a persistent background, which I'll have to learn to live with. During the lightning-fast ride I don't look at the road, I don't care how long we take. For the first time in I don't know how long I feel like chatting.

I didn't know that Antonio had an eighteen-year-old daughter, I've never before heard him laugh, but I hear it now in response to a joke of mine about young girls nowadays. "A constant worry," I add, talking the way a father would talk. And he knows he can trust what I say, after all, I've known a lot of girls in my life. I don't know how long he's been parked outside our office building, but when the conversation runs down and he throws me one of his questioning glances, I get out of the car and prepare to face my last day at work.

I go in through the glass door, knowing that it's the last time I'll do so in my official role. Everyone is immediately struck by the way I'm dressed. Paola quickly closes the fashion magazine she's been leafing through and gives me one of those contrite, pained looks that pass for condolences.

Then it's Elena's turn. The same look. The same words, too, as if it's the protocol. Apart from a few additions: "The meeting is fixed for five. I have to admit I was afraid you wouldn't be here in time. But you're early for once."

"Why? What time is it?"

"Four. You're lucky there wasn't a lot of traffic from the airport, it's usually chock-a-block at this time of day. Take all the time you need."

And she leaves me alone in the room.

I should feel relieved, but I stay on my guard, I know all Your changing moods by now.

In a few hours of my time, this problem will be completely out of the way. I can't deny that there's a touch of bitterness in this final look around my office. After all, until not so long ago, this place was my life. A small part of my consciousness, the part which up till now has found nourishment in ambition and social recognition, continues to clamour inside me, telling me I should consider all this a defeat.

I unplug the intercom, so that Elena won't be able to disturb me, then lower the blinds and switch off the light. I want to be in the dark, sitting in my armchair. For a few minutes I try to sink into the silence, knowing that it's only apparent, because behind that door there's a world that never stops, that keeps on producing, keeps on churning out money. I kept on track as long as I could, but now I've got off.

Suddenly the door opens and light floods the room.

Elena, with her five minutes' head start and her head full of things to remember, stands there in the doorway. Once again, I've managed to surprise her. She wasn't expecting me to be in the dark, or to look so calm, or to be smiling slightly.

"I'm sorry, I didn't mean to disturb you," she says almost hesitantly, "everyone's been looking for you, and there are appointments to fix."

"Later, Elena," I say, rising from the armchair to leave the room. "Later."

I start wandering through the offices, without a specific aim, I get lots of puzzled glances, a few polite greetings, the usual predictable condolences.

Another wave of condolences awaits me in the conference room. The director utters some polite phrases, without getting up from his chair. In his eyes he still has the unease he had the last time we met, and he can't hold back a grimace of indignation, I assume because of my totally inappropriate clothing. But because of the situation, he can't make any comments.

Barbara is sitting to his right, which means she'll be the one to take my place very soon. She greets me with a slight smile, then her lips narrow and her nostrils flare in that characteristic way of hers that makes her look like a reptile.

Nobody mentions my father any more, because Righini has entered the room and sat down on the other side of the table. It's time to tackle more important matters.

"You got here early," Righini says to me. "It's always an unknown quantity, a meeting with you, or am I mistaken?"

The director quickly intervenes to change the subject. I've never seen him so obsequious and accommodating. Christ, he's gagging for a signature. His gestures ooze impatience. I sympathize with him. I'll soon be a mutineer, but he's the ship's master, the commander, the responsibility is his, if anything goes wrong he'll be the last one to abandon ship.

I used to accept all his decisions without batting an eyelid. I was like the others, I had the same smile Barbara has now when she pretends to have caught one of his jokes, and I carried out orders, trying, whenever possible, to anticipate his desires. I was part of the court, driven by the need for a secular faith, perhaps, for someone to believe in blindly. And my happiness, our happiness, depended on the director.

After this rapid and occasionally incomprehensible meeting, we find ourselves alone, the director and I, in his office. This time I'm ready: without even giving him time to open his mouth I tell him I'm resigning.

At first he seems incredulous, perhaps even a little relieved. He tries placing responsibility for what's happening on my father's death, he tells me that things will settle down, that I'll get back on track, but they are empty words and we both know it. I'm not ready to retrace my steps, and the firm can't afford to wait for me.

Then, for the first time since I've known him, the director lowers his eyes as a sign of surrender.

"I did all I could for you," he says. "I taught you the business, the way I would have done for my son. I was sure we'd do great things together. I thought of you as my winning card, and for a while you were, Romano. We've had our successes…"

I'm sorry to see that he's still keeping his distance from me—and even sorrier that the fact that he's just concluded such an important deal is helping to cushion the blow for him. There's no sadness in his eyes, just a programme he knows he has to keep to. He's probably planned on giving me another five minutes, ten at the most, then he'll dismiss me, putting off other matters for another time.

I never thought it would be so informal and hurried. In any case, I can't wait to leave this place. There are games you feel liberated in losing.

A few moments later I find myself back in my car. I don't want to know what time it is, or how much time I have left before it gets dark. I just want to get to the sea.

Antonio raises no objections, he smiles and starts the car. "Is the beach at Fregene OK?"

I nod, with a sigh. A few hours ago I saw it from the window of the plane. There it was below me, flat, shining in the sunlight, so infinite as to make me feel dizzy, and it seemed like an invitation to hope.

During the ride, Antonio and I chat a bit more. Before getting out, I tell him that I'll miss his company and that we should have talked more.

"We can still remedy that," he says.

"Not so easy," I object. "In a few days we'll be saying goodbye for good. I'm leaving the company, let's hope they give you somebody who's less of a bastard." Then, as he watches incredulously, I get out and walk down to the beach.

The first thing I do is take off my shoes and socks. My feet sink into the sand, anxious to let every single grain run through them. A breeze smelling of fish and salt tickles my face, this sea reminds me of my childhood. Now, as then, the sky is slowly turning pink, and here I am, waiting for the sunset. Something tells me that this time it won't be too fast, and that it'll be quite moving, as it was on those long August days.

The wind becomes more intense, the waves swell before breaking on the shore. I remember my father's words, written in pen, on the back of that photograph: "You can't beat the wave. Salvation is inside you."

That wave is like time. And we are on a journey, cargo ships sailing to an unknown destination, entirely at the mercy of the crew. The parts of the ship communicate through the manifestation of symptoms. Sometimes reactions can be externally stimulated: you just need to use a certain kind of substance to transform your perception of time and space, and prepare to veer abruptly in another direction. At other times, the stimulus comes from inside: the burden of a choice—how best to get through those waves, how to prepare to face the storm—can create a great upheaval on the bridge, the fear of shipwreck. And the restlessness and instability on that bridge—our mind—soon manifests itself. That's where I started to imagine You as an old man determined to destroy me, when in fact You were inviting me to dig beneath the surface of things, moving back and forth between moral and material, between concrete and imaginary, between long-lasting and ephemeral. And everything started when You stopped with her. De Santis was right, the mind can do incredible things.

I lie down on the sand and close my eyes. I feel as if I'm exhausted after a long run, and I can almost see him, my father, as I've never seen him before. He's waiting for me at the finishing line, with a smile. He wants me to stop, he wants me to realize I've left the most important things behind. I feel my little days going back light years beyond the horizon, and I see myself, tiny, at grips with urgent, predictable banalities, in search of a non-existent perfection, in a ridiculous enterprise, devoid of foundation, constantly turned to a pre-programmed future, a path strewn with objectives. And suddenly I feel as if I've finally managed to throw off the weight of all this. It wasn't time that was running fast, but my life. And it wasn't time that stopped, but my eyes, that day at the airport, when they came to rest on her face, which told me something I didn't yet know about myself, or that I had only forgotten.

When I open my eyes again, the surface of the sea on the horizon is pink, interrupted by the flight of a few fleeting seagulls. The sun is melting between the waves, like a snowball on a summer's day. So slowly. I've just re-emerged on the backs of the wave, to follow it wherever it decides to lead me.

Antonio joins me on the beach. "May I?"

And he sits down next to me.

"I'm sorry you're going, I wanted to tell you."

I smile, I could reply that I'm sorry too, but my extraordinary calm would contradict me.

He is about to stand up again, but I stop him. "Stay, if you like."

He sits down again and there we stay for a while, in silence, looking at the sea. Me and my Charon, the man who until today barely had a face.

"I never noticed it in all this time," he says after a while, looking at my hair.

"What?"

"That tattoo, there, behind your neck, it's easier to see when you're wearing a T-shirt. I didn't have you down as someone who'd go in for tattoos."

I frown. "Actually I'm not. And I don't know what you're talking about."

"There's something written there," Antonio insists. "A bit faded, but there are definitely words." The sound of Isabelle's laughter echoes in my head, I see the amusement in her eyes as she holds the marker in her hand.

"May I?" Antonio asks. He reaches out a hand, moves my T-shirt slightly and reads: "*For ever... never.* That's what's written: *For ever never.* What does it mean?"

Memories are like taste, sometimes you need only a slight hint for a whole world to open up to you, an infinite echo chamber. Isabelle lying on my bed, me with my head on her belly, like a castaway washed up on a beach. There are love affairs that remain inside you for ever, even though you'll never experience them, she said, and she wrote it on my skin. There are love affairs that are like cloaks, they keep us warm, they protect us, and there is something magical about them, as if they could go beyond the borders of time and space and never come to an end. They are like moments that imprint themselves in our memories, leaving you grateful that you have had them, whatever happens.

"For ever never. It's a paradox. What does it mean?"

Smiling at his curiosity, I turn and nod: "That's just it, it's a paradox."

A moment later I get to my feet. "Take me back to the city, Antonio. I'll ask you one last favour: don't take me home, drop me in the Campo de' Fiori."

19

ISABELLE MUST ALREADY have put Giulia to bed by now, maybe she's reading a book. When I say goodbye to Antonio, closing the car door behind me, I have the taste in my mouth of things postponed, made even more bitter by the smell of my father on the sweatshirt I'm wearing. I force myself to walk to her front door, I owe it to myself to confront her, now, and to strip myself naked, to ask her for a second chance.

Maybe she'll invent an excuse, she'll certainly insist that I leave, but I can't give up yet, not before I've told her my story. A story of time racing, of a life that can't keep up with it and a new love that's able to slow it down.

In the late evening, the square has divested itself of its frills and is bathed in the golden light of the street lamps. The front door is closed. I'm about to press the button by the entryphone, but before I have time a man rushes out, allowing me to slip inside. Better that way. It'll be easier to try and convince her when we're looking each other in the eyes.

As I climb the stairs of the building my legs are shaking, because I'm afraid, just as I always am when I'm about to see her again.

One, two, three…

Abruptly I stop counting.

I don't need to get to five any more.

I ring the bell. The neighbours' dog has started barking. "Pablo, stop it!" its mistress immediately yells at it.

Isabelle comes to the door. She sees me through the spyhole, and I sense that she gives a start. "What are you doing here at this hour?"

"I need to talk to you. Please, open the door."

She half opens the door without taking off the chain. She's in a nightdress and dressing gown. Her eyes are cold. "It's late," she says in a trembling voice. "Giulia's asleep and I was just about to join her. Please, Svevo, go away."

"No, I can't."

"Why are you doing this?"

"I told you, Isabelle, you're in my blood," and I feel fear relaxing its grip.

Her eyes become watery.

I take a deep breath. "Since I met you, so many things have happened… I don't even know where to start… Maybe with that day at the airport. When I saw you…"

"When was this?"

"A few months ago. You were on your way to Paris with Giulia. We saw each other just before getting on. I asked you if you needed a hand to carry your case…"

She remembers, I'm sure, but she continues to keep her distance. "I don't know where you're going with this."

"For a start, I'd like to come in."

"Svevo, it's late."

"No, it isn't late. It would be late if I left. And if I look back, it seems to me all I've ever done in my life is leave. My father died three days ago…" And as I say this, the image of his coffin parades in front of my eyes, and I realize only now that it really happened. I see my grief reflected in her eyes, which open wide in surprise, and in the features of her face, which crumple in a grimace of sorrow. She's about to take off the chain, but I stop her, taking her hand in mine. "Give me just a few minutes, Isabelle. I don't want your compassion, I want your respect. I'm not proud of what my life was and I can't hide it from you. Maybe you deserve a simpler story, someone capable of loving you without complications. I don't know what love is, I've never believed in it. But I believed in you from the first moment I saw you. In your power to change me, to make me see things in a different way. I can't turn back, without first insisting... I want to try my hardest for you, Isabelle. I don't want to harm you, and I could never harm your daughter, above all I don't want to leave anything unresolved, any loves 'for ever and never'. Time doesn't forgive, and I can't risk regretting this moment: the promises I could have made you, the words I should have said to you. I've accumulated too many heavy silences, I won't leave without first telling you what I think..."

As I speak, her hand reacts to my touch until her fingers intertwine with mine. I see her yield little by little, her eyes turn large and round and full of hope. She takes off the chain as I continue to speak, and looks at me, but I know that her mind has flown ahead, to the consequences of this choice. "Just give me a few minutes..." I say again, and find her lips pressed to mine. She hugs me tight, tighter, then moves back to let me into the apartment. Her kisses are like promises, she wants to give me more than a few minutes, she might even be mad enough to grant me a whole lifetime.

When I close the door of her apartment behind me, I know that Isabelle will carry me with her to the place where moments have no time, and I know that happiness tastes like her lips and the tears bathing her cheeks. It smells like her hair and sounds like my thoughts, as I close my eyes, wanting this night never to end.

20

Sometime later

I T'S ONE MORNING in March.

I am asleep when I feel a wet tongue start moving up and down my cheek. I recognize him from his breath, which smells of hard biscuits: it's Bengo, the Beretton family dog.

Isabelle's mother calls him in French from the corridor. He freezes for a moment, throws me a last puzzled look, then in the end decides to jump down off the bed, disarranging the mattress in the process.

I'm in Paris. And I'm cured.

Isabelle would be able to sleep even if bombs were falling in the street: she's motionless, a mask over her eyes, her red curls covering half her face. Traces of Bengo everywhere, he must have tried that little trick with his tongue on her, too, but in vain. And yet I know it would only take a few soft words in her ear, whispered in a certain way, to wake her with a start. I can't help it, it always amuses me.

She jerks up like a spring. "What's happening?" she cries, moving her arms under the blankets. Then she recognizes the room, realizes she's in her parents' apartment for the weekend and turns to me, a look of surprise still on her face. The mask now covers only one eye, and her mouth is wide open. She's funny.

We're in love. She's untidy, distracted, I'm fussy, a pain in the arse, and yet we're in love.

She's always leaving her clothes scattered on the floor, but her untidiness is bearable. I think I know her most intimate thoughts, and I like them. I trust her smiles, they would never be capable of doing me harm. What I know of her is enough for me, sometimes I even anticipate her moves. Habit has made us complicit with each other. For example, I know that in winter she likes to go into the bathroom barefoot, even though the tiles are cold, because then she appreciates the warmth of the bed even more. She's one of those people who never take anything for granted, and has never demanded to be happy. Sometimes I get the absurd, crazy thought that she could melt into the air at any moment, like a vision. She's my angel. She saved my life, and she might take flight again now that her mission is complete.

"Think that's funny, eh?" she says, adjusting her hair and taking off the mask. She threatens to make me pay for it.

"I'm so scared," I reply, not scared at all.

"It'll happen when you least expect it, you'll see." She jumps out of bed and looks for her slippers. She says they're always getting away from her, as if slippers could get away. "Don't forget we have to pick up your aunt from the airport. She's landing at eight tonight."

"She's not an idiot, and besides, she's with her children, they can take a taxi."

"Let's go and pick them up anyway."

But at about five, before going to the airport, we find ourselves walking along the Seine. Isabelle is wearing a beige coat with a white fur collar, she could have stepped straight out of a painting. The sky has taken on a weary look, the blue has faded and on the horizon brush-strokes of grey seem to make it even sleepier.

Giulia is in front of us. She rushed forward a few metres, and now she's slowed down. She's become a beautiful little girl. She smiles at the sight of the line of miniature Eiffel Towers on a rug a street vendor has laid in front of him. She looks at them, grabs them, studies them. She wants them. And we haven't yet learnt to say no to her, at least not about things of little account.

Isabelle's hand is intertwined with mine, her warmth in marked contrast to the sharp late-afternoon wind. Our rings rub together, almost as if they wanted to melt into one another. I turn up the collar of my coat with my free hand as we turn on to the Pont des Arts and walk across the worn wooden planks that creak almost imperceptibly beneath our feet. Giulia follows us, skipping, laughing, talking, asking questions, calling us. Her mother humours her with a patience that's beyond me, the same patience that stunned me that afternoon, when I saw her at the airport for the first time. And now, as only she knows how, she again unsettles me as she leans on the iron railing and turns to look at the Seine, the Île de la Cité, the grim Conciergerie, and gazes in admiration at this City of Light which is almost dreamlike, veiled as it is by the diffuse light of the hour.

"My God, Svevo. Look at this place."

It's the place where she was born and grew up, her place. And now it's as if she's looking at her whole life on the horizon, such is the emotion I see in her eyes.

I know that she would have liked her camera with her and that she can't bear the idea that she left it at home for one afternoon.

The light is perfect, the colours unrepeatable. She looks at me, then at the scene, then again at me, and at last realizes that she doesn't need a camera: this scene has impressed itself on her mind just as it would on a photograph.

I remember to check my e-mails on my mobile phone, there are reservations for the villa in Cortona to confirm. In the end Isabelle convinced me to transform it into a little hotel, and basically she was right, we couldn't have managed with all those free rooms. To furnish it, we didn't use a designer. She handled it all, adapting old objects she found in the cellar. So now even in Cortona we have a refrigerator transformed into a dresser, and an old sewing machine functions as a bedside table. You certainly can't say that the villa has no personality, or that it isn't a hospitable place, otherwise I wouldn't find myself so often having breakfast with people from all over the world and listening to their stories. Most of them are artists: apparently the countryside around it is a much-prized source of inspiration, I was told by a painter who couldn't stop contemplating it, until he bought a canvas and started painting it, prolonging his stay by several months.

Isabelle takes the mobile from my hands, her smile is trying to tell me that there is time for everything. There are so many things with which we can fill our life, the prow of that cargo ship without destination. So many books still unread, songs unheard, places not yet explored. So many departures, so many returns. There are days, like this one, when the hands of my watch stand at midday, giving me the illusion we still have the whole day ahead of us, even when the sun is about to set. But time evaporates every day and you can't dilute it, or stop it, only fill it. Technology can help a bit, though sometimes it ends up swallowing us. These days you can have everything in an instant, and yet I know people who would give everything away to have one moment. One like this, for example: the three of us, strolling hand in hand on the Pont des Arts.

There is a band in the middle of the bridge. A heterogeneous group of people playing a blues: a pot-bellied sixty-year-old man in a red-and-white tracksuit on trombone, a couple of young boys in jeans on trumpet, a lady in a Fifties-style check suit on saxophone, and two strange characters on drums and guitar, one with yellow-and-blue trousers and the other in camouflage fatigues. They're all different, and all smiling. They seem to have come together in this place by chance, like the rest of us, we stop to listen to them and find it impossible to keep still. I wonder what their story is, who they were before they turned into this little band, maybe only for a day, and in their eyes I find mine. We're like Isabelle's objects: refrigerators becoming dressers, cribs turned into window boxes.

Giulia calls to her mother from the middle of the bridge, because she wants her to dance with her. Isabelle tries to resist, but then yields and goes to her, slightly embarrassed, laughing, without taking her eyes off me.

The girl imitates her mother's steps, and she's so comical, some of the onlookers can't help applauding, and nor can I. Then I grab Isabelle by the waist and start dancing with her, and she stops laughing and looks at me. She looks at me as if she wants to tell me how much she loves me. But I know that, just as I know that I'd like to bring into the world a child with her eyes, that all the richness of this life could be encompassed in a dance like this, that my hands are shaking, that Giulia is pulling my coat, that everyone is watching us, and that I love my wife more than ever.

I know it, just as I know that time devours everything, but not these memories, not this love, not the moments that last for ever.

Acknowledgements

So here I am, thanking those who made this "new" adventure possible (I say "new", even though I started writing this story nearly ten years ago), those who held my hand on this treacherous path.

I will start with my nearest and dearest: parents, siblings, friends and relatives. Those who love me are sure to know who I mean. Thank you to all those who racked their brains along with me to come up with a title. To the colleagues who inspired me, my schools and teachers. Next, thank you to Raffaele, Carol, Antonella and the team at Newton who continue to support me. A special thank you to Paolo Taggi, for all his invaluable advice, and to the Coccaglioni family, who ten years ago allowed me to start to dream.

A thank you from the bottom of my heart to a great man who flew up to heaven too early: Oscar, an angel and a true friend.

And a small thank you to Massimo, who told me one evening about a belly button and the fear of getting lost.